I0679840

The

Kind

Redemption

by Alan Maas

The Kind Legacy Series — Book 2

ACKNOWLEDGMENTS

Special thanks to the Staff and Owners of the Frawley Ranches Inc. (Elkhorn Ridge Resort) for the use of their images and access to their land. Please visit https://elkhornridgeresort.com/history for more information on the ranch and to schedule a visit.

Published by Alan Maas

ISBN: 979-8-9890660-4-9

Printed in the United States of America

Dedication

I would like to dedicate this book to my friends and family—without them, none of this would have been possible.

Too often, we take the people closest to us for granted, when in truth, it's their presence that shapes the experiences of our lives. I have truly been blessed.

My parents took on the incredible challenge of raising five children, each of whom turned out exceptional in their own ways. I know not everyone is fortunate enough to have strong family bonds or lifelong friendships, but I encourage you: don't give up on the people who can walk alongside you, lift you up, and share your journey.

Through this book and the Thoen Stone Tours, I've been fortunate to make new friends, and I look forward to making many more. Thank you all for being part of this adventure.

If you'd like to hear more from the Kinds, I'd love to hear from you.

— Alan Maas

From the Author

I hope you enjoyed *The Kind Whisper* and are excited to dive into *The Kind Redemption*. The next installment picks up right where the first left off—deepening the mystery and following Eli Kind's search for truth.

Thank you for being part of the journey.

—Alan Maas

Contents

Prologue

Eli Kind stood at the edge of Centennial Valley, gazing toward the hills that had shaped his family's fate. His hands were roughened by work, his mind burdened by questions left unanswered. The mystery of his missing uncle, Ezra, had gnawed at him for years, but now the search was more than just a personal journey—it was a path that would lead him deep into the heart of his family's legacy. A legacy intertwined with the legend of the Thoen Stone and a secret too powerful to remain buried.

Though the Kind and Anderson ranches flourished, the encroaching Gold Rush and the promise of riches had brought more than just miners into the area. The land was filling with men—some seeking fortune, others seeking justice—and more than a few seeking revenge. Eli knew that the answers to his questions were as buried as the treasures of the hills themselves, but he was determined to find them, no matter the cost.

In the town of Deadwood, where the echoes of Wild Bill Hickok's gunshot still lingered in the air, new alliances would be forged, and old ghosts would rise from the shadows. Eli's search would lead him into the paths of historical figures—Teddy Roosevelt, Seth Bullock, and even the legendary Crazy Horse. Each step brought him closer to the truth, and yet, each turn in the road left him questioning what he believed was real.

Was the Kind family bound by fate—or by a curse?

The winds of the past were stirring, and the land called to Eli, urging him forward. But with every discovery, the line between friend and foe blurred, and he would soon learn that some truths come with a cost.

And sometimes, redemption isn't just about finding the past—it's about confronting it.

About the Author

Alan Maas is a historical fiction author with a deep appreciation for the untold stories of the American frontier. Drawing inspiration from real events, forgotten legends, and his passion for the Black Hills region, Maas brings the past to life through richly imagined characters and immersive, atmospheric storytelling.

History has always fascinated me—not for the dates and numbers, which never seemed to stick, but for the stories and the way everything connects. My goal is to write stories that weave history together, making it both educational and entertaining. Every time I uncover a new piece of history; I'm amazed at how it always ties back to something we can relate to—often in ways that surprise me.

That said, research is key. There are always multiple sides to every story, and understanding the full picture requires digging deeper. As I always say, never pass up the chance to have a conversation or listen to a story—you never know where it might lead or what you'll discover!

The Kind Redemption – Character List

The Kind Family

- **Eli Kind** – Main character; surveyor, miner, lawman, rancher.
- **Christina Kind** – Eli's wife; daughter of James and Catherine Anderson (*The Kind Whisper*).
- **Ezra Kind** – Eli's long-lost uncle.
- **Daniel Kind** – Son of Eli and Christina Kind.
- **Richard Kind** – Eli's uncle; soldier and farmer.

Historical Figures & Lawmen

- **Seth Bullock** – Sheriff of Deadwood and businessman.
- **Theodore Roosevelt** – Rancher and politician.
- **Sol Star** – Seth Bullock's partner and mayor of Deadwood.
- **General Nelson Miles** – Commander of the Military Division of the Missouri.
- **Colonel James W. Forsyth** – Commander of the Seventh Cavalry at Wounded Knee.
- **Lieutenant Dunbar** – Lieutenant in the 7th Cavalry.
- **Dr. Valentine McGillycuddy** – Eli's friend; doctor and Indian Agent.
- **Fanny McGillycuddy** – Dr. McGillycuddy's wife.

The Roosevelt Ranch Hands

- **Bill Sewall** – Cowboy and ranch hand for Theodore Roosevelt.
- **Wilmot "Will" Dow** – Cowboy and ranch hand for Theodore Roosevelt.
- **Tom Crandell** – Cowboy and ranch hand for Theodore Roosevelt.
- **Whitey** – Cowboy and ranch hand for Theodore Roosevelt.

Native American Characters

- **Tȟamila (Bloody Knife)** – Friend of Eli and Whitey.
- **Skau** – Tȟamila's mother.
- **Kȟaŋǧí** – Tȟamila's father.

Merager Family & Associates

- **Kurtis Merager** – Sawmill owner; husband to Jillian.
- **Jillian Merager** – Teacher; wife to Kurtis.

Trappers, Miners & Businessmen

- **Mollie DeLacompt** – Wife of Joseph DeLacompt (of the Thoen Stone).
- **G.W. Wood ("Woody")** – Name found on the Thoen Stone.
- **Harris Franklin** – Prominent businessman in Deadwood.
- **Tom Wellington** – Owner of the Belle Fourche livestock auction company.
- **Scotty Phillips** – Buffalo rancher.
- **John Cashner** – Hardware store owner displaying the Thoen Stone.
- **Louis Thoen** – Stonemason who discovered the Thoen Stone.
- **Ferdinand Turgeon** – Neighbor of the Andersons.

Friends & Associates

- **Henry Frawley** – Lawyer and landowner; friend of Eli.
- **Calamity Jane** – Frontierswoman; friend of Eli.

The Kind Redemption – Timeline of Events

- **1874** – The Custer Expedition explores the Black Hills; Eli participates.
- **1875** – Eli leaves the army and joins the Newton–Jenny Expedition.
- **1876** – The Black Hills Gold Rush begins; Wild Bill Hickok is killed in Deadwood. Battle of Little Bighorn.
- **1877** - George Hearst purchases the Homestake Mine, He bought the claim from the Manuel brothers, Fred and Moses, and it was named Homestake.
- **1876–1877** – Eli marries Christina Anderson; the Kind Stagehouse is built and becomes a successful enterprise. Daniel Kind is born
- **1885**- Teddy Roosevelt builds the Elkhorn Ranch house
- **1887** – The Thoen Stone is discovered by stonemason Louis Thoen, renewing interest in the mystery of Ezra Kind.
- **1890** – Wounded Knee Battle

Chapter 1 – The Long Road Home

After sending messages at the Western Union station—one to his uncle Richard in Minnesota and another to his wife Christina letting her know he was headed back to the ranch—Eli prepared for the long, four-day ride home. He knew it would give him plenty of time to think. He wished he could've taken the note Mollie DeLacompt had shown him, but it was one of the last possessions of her late husband, and he could see it meant a lot to her. Instead, Eli copied the words onto the back of the paper he'd used for his message to Richard.

As he rode west, the bluffs of the Missouri River gradually hid Fort Pierre from view. It was late April, and Eli knew the nights would be cold; he planned to ride into the night to stay warm and rest when the morning sun brought warmth.

His thoughts kept returning to what Mollie had told him: if her husband, Joseph DeLacompt, had returned from the Black Hills, could there be others? He pulled out the paper he'd used to rub over the stone, now knowing it bore his uncle Ezra's carving. He read the names aloud:

"Came to these hills in 1833, seven of us:
DeLacompt
Ezra Kind
G.W. Wood
T. Brown
R. Kent
Wm. King
Indian Crow
All dead but me, Ezra Kind. Killed by ind[ians] beyond the high hill. Got our gold June 1834."

"Someone must know what happened," he murmured to himself, carefully folding the paper and tucking it into his saddlebag as the last light of day faded. The gentle sway of his horse lulled him into a trance until he realized he was growing cold and could barely see the road. He'd reached the Cheyenne River, and he wasn't about to attempt a cold, nighttime crossing.

After watering his horse, Eli staked her by some new grass sprouting from the spring thaw, then gathered firewood. As he warmed himself by the fire and ate jerky and bread—kindly provided by Mrs. DeLacompt—he quickly drifted into sleep, waking only when the warm sunlight stirred him.

"Time to get moving," Eli said to his horse. After both had a drink, he faced the cold crossing. The spring runoff made the river swift, the water a murky, clay-brown. Remembering the shallow route used by wagon trains, he guided his horse across. Once they'd dried off, Eli took out the messages from the Western Union station, starting with the one he'd sent to Christina. Reading it aloud, he half-expected his horse to listen.

"Dearest Christina, I have so much to tell you when I get home. This was a good trip. I miss you and can't wait to see you! I should be there in four days. Love, Eli."

"What do you think, Ginger?" he asked his horse. "Is that enough for now?" He looked at her, smiling. "I don't know much more myself—just more questions, and those cost too much to send. Besides, I'll tell her everything when I get home. She'll help settle my wandering mind." Ginger's slow head bob seemed like a nod of approval, so he switched to the message for his uncle Richard and the verses from the paper Mollie had shown him. He read them aloud too.

"Joseph DeLacompt
Ezra Kind
We came for the gold

12

We are going to be rich
We are going to help our families
We are going to buy land."

"I think Mollie was right—this must have been something Uncle Ezra was teaching Joe," he mused, looking down at Ginger. He then took out the etching from the stone that Louis Thoen had found, noticing again the handwriting matched that on the paper. "It has to be Uncle Ezra who wrote them both!" Ginger's nod made Eli smile, and they picked up the pace, both eager to get home.

As evening set in, Eli found a small creek for a rest. While gathering firewood and warming some jerky, he thought about Mollie's story of her late husband's partner, whom she called "Woody." Talking aloud, he chuckled, then turned to Ginger. "I wonder how much you actually listen to me—or care. My wife probably wonders the same thing," he laughed, propping his jerky over a rock to warm it by the fire.

After his modest supper, Eli lay back on his saddle, watching Ginger graze in the moonlight. Suddenly, he grabbed his saddlebags, pulling out the etching from the stone. He looked at the name under Ezra's: "G.W. Wood."

"That has to be Woody!" he exclaimed; startling Ginger awake. "Sorry, Ginger," he soothed. "But don't you think it has to be him?" He pointed at the paper, laughing to himself at her lack of response.

Morning came quickly, and as the cold dawn urged him to move, Eli's thoughts returned to G.W. Wood, or "Woody." He felt resolved enough to head back to Fort Pierre for answers but pressed on, eager to get home. Just as he neared Fort Meade, another thought surfaced: Mollie had mentioned a place called Whisper Gulch, where Joe had urged her to go on his deathbed. Eli had never heard of it, but it had to be near where the stone was found. He promised himself he'd start his search there.

As he and Ginger crested the last hill, Fort Meade came into view, bustling with evening chores. The barracks were lit, and he could hear a band practicing the same song over and over. Recognizing *The Star-Spangled Banner*, Eli recalled it being played frequently during his time with the Seventh Cavalry in the Black Hills. As Ginger's ears perked, Eli leaned forward and murmured, "I guess that's our welcome home?"

Ginger's pace quickened as Eli's thoughts drifted to the comrades he had lost at the Battle of Little Big Horn. He recalled that the only survivor of the battle had been brought to Fort Meade—Captain Keogh's horse, Comanche. Eli had once intended to visit the fort to see the legendary horse, but now, as the memories weighed on him, he wondered if it was best to leave the past where it lay. After all, had he extended his enlistment by just one more year, he too would have been among the fallen.

Approaching Sturgis, Eli debated stopping for supplies in "Scooptown," as soldiers called it. But his urge to get home—and Ginger's eagerness for a comfy barn—kept him on the trail. They passed the quiet town of Whitewood and finally reached the Anderson ranch. Seeing a faint light in the barn and in the upstairs of the house, Eli's thoughts turned to Christina. Ginger broke into a faster gait, eager to reach home, but Eli reined her in. "Easy, girl. No need to rush," he said with a grin.

Ginger made her way straight to the barn, and Eli quickly unsaddled her, leaving his tack on the ground. Tossing some hay into the manger, he hurried toward the house, his pace hindered by saddle stiffness. Just as he reached the door, it swung open, and Christina leapt into his arms. She kissed him deeply, then said, "I heard the commotion in the barn and just knew it was you! I would have come out to help, but I was finishing up the dishes."

Eli returned her kiss, then whispered, "I missed you so much. I'm glad to be home. Now, let's go inside—I've had enough of the outdoors." With a wink, he added, "And I have a lot to tell you."

She smiled, glancing at the kitchen where the leftover roast waited. "No, you didn't miss it—I was just about to put it in the icebox. You made good time!"

"Yes, I did. I couldn't spend another night without you." He winked again and nodded toward the bedroom. She lowered her voice. "As you can see, we have guests."

Eli grinned, leaning in. "I noticed. I'll mind my manners…mostly." Taking her hand, he led her into the bedroom, sighing with relief as he closed the door.

Chapter 2 – Home on the Range

The morning seemed to come quickly, but waking up beside his bride made Eli feel the night had been well spent. He could tell Christina was restless, eager to get up and start breakfast for the guests, but he tried to pull her closer as she squirmed free.

"Mr. Kind, you know I have to get breakfast going!" Christina pleaded.

"I know, but I still haven't had enough of you to make up for the time I've been away," Eli replied.

"We should have an empty house tonight," Christina whispered in his ear, "and we can catch up on everything."

"Okay, I'm holding you to that," Eli said with a grin.

"Are you going to tell me more about your trip?" Christina asked as she got ready for her day.

"Yes," Eli answered, "though I think I have even more questions now than when I left. I'm still trying to make sense of it all. I'll fill you in after breakfast and the morning chores."

As he dressed, Eli looked around the bedroom, reflecting on his work on the Kind Stagehouse. There was still work to do, but it had already become a popular spot for travelers and even some town folk looking for a quick getaway. After all, the stagehouse was the first place in the area with running water and plumbing. No more carrying the toilet seat from the wood stove to the outhouse! Having endured enough of that both in the army and on his family's Minnesota farm, Eli had crafted a water tank for the house's lookout tower and piped the water into the closets upstairs and downstairs. He even installed coils on the back of the kitchen stove, so Christina could have hot water, running it into the clawfoot tub he'd bought her as a wedding gift.

Eli's inventiveness could be seen throughout the stagehouse. He'd designed the master bedroom adjacent to the kitchen but not beneath the guest rooms upstairs, which reduced noise from above while allowing the morning kitchen sounds to wake the guests. As Eli put it, "Get them moving down the trail!" The lobby, or sitting room, off the kitchen served as a cozy spot where guests and the Kinds could wind down after a long day on the trail or the ranch. Christina had chosen two davenports adorned with tassels, jewels, and pillows—accessories Eli never quite understood. The davenports were accented by a rocking chair and matching "soft chairs," as Eli called them. In this room, the guests also dined at the table, enjoying the meals Christina prepared, with occasional help from Eli.

The staircase at the other end of the room led out to the covered front porch. Christina and Eli spent many evenings swinging on the porch swing Eli had built, and it was the first-place guests wandered to on warm evenings. Upstairs, with oak banisters imported from Chicago, there were four guest rooms, each unique, with different setups and bed sizes to accommodate various guests. Eli placed the water closet between the two north rooms, making them slightly smaller, while a double wash sink on the south wall provided quick access to running water. Guests often marveled at the convenience of such "fancy waterworks," which were all possible thanks to the tower Eli built at the back of the house. The tower was the tallest part of the house, with a 500-gallon water tank at the top, kept full by a windmill pump near the barn. Eli's pride in the tower was evident; he never missed a chance to tell guests how he'd used pulleys to lift the tank to the top. The tower also served as a lookout over the northern, southern, and western pastures—the eastern land wasn't part of the ranch- yet.

The stagehouse was Eli's dream, and its earnings from stage guests and occasional lodgers were steadily funding his goal of buying more land for the ranch, particularly on the eastern side. His father's words often echoed in his mind: "The land can take care of you for a lifetime."

Though money was tight, the stagehouse was thriving, and leasing land for grazing horses needed for the stage line and local communities kept their finances steady. Christina's family also helped, and business dealings with Henry Frawley, a local lawyer, provided valuable support. Henry was well-connected, not only in law but also in land, merchandise, and even gold. One of his connections with the Kinds involved the stage barns on the southern edge of the Kind ranch.

The Stagehouse

One evening, while Eli was designing the stagehouse, Henry stopped by on one of his frequent trips from Spearfish to Deadwood, where his law office was located. Eli had been expecting him, hoping to get his opinion on a few things. During that visit, Henry convinced Eli that to complete his dream, he'd need to provide for the reinsmen and the teams that pulled the stagecoaches. Eli had intended to manage with just the stagehouse barn, but after a few drinks, Henry persuaded him to build a dedicated stage barn instead. The barn became the talk of the Stageline: it was large enough to fit two coaches under partial cover, with a pulley system Eli designed that made unhooking the teams and storing tack in the nearby tack room easy. The reinsmen even had a comfortable bunkhouse just steps away from their coach and team.

Henry had been right—the stage companies paid extra, ensuring the Kind Stagehouse was a designated stop. Henry and Eli made a good team, and their evening meetings led to even more ideas, including acquiring additional land through the Homestead Act. They often found homesteaders who hadn't improved upon their land or couldn't make it work. Through Henry's practice, which kept records of local deeds, they were able to identify such properties, and soon these homesteaders realized that selling land they hadn't paid much for was better than leaving empty-handed. With Frawley's help, Eli and Henry saw that land ownership in Centennial Valley was becoming more than a dream.

The Stagebarns

Chapter 3 – Catching Up

Time at the Stagehouse seemed to fly by, but Eli knew he needed to make time for Christina. They tried to reserve Friday nights as "their" time, though unexpected guests sometimes made that impossible. This Friday, however, Eli was determined to have the evening to themselves. He hadn't yet had a chance to tell Christina about his trip to Fort Pierre or the thoughts lingering in his mind about his missing uncle.

Eli and Christina decided to spend Friday evening down by the creek near the Stagebarn bunkhouse. While building the Stagebarn, Eli had often taken breaks under the oak trees along the creek bank, where he eventually set up a bench and a small table fashioned from a broken wagon wheel. This spot became their retreat from the bustle of the Stagehouse. With a full house of guests that week—mostly from Spearfish—Eli knew the bunkhouse would be empty if the weather turned on them.

Eli helped Christina pack their supper into a basket and took it out to the buggy, which he'd hitched up outside the door. Normally, they would walk, but he wanted to add a touch of romance to the evening, and with spring weather still chilly, a ride would be warmer than a late-night walk back. Christina noticed his extra effort and smiled. Finally, he would have a chance to share the full story of his trip without interruptions.

After placing the basket in the back of the buggy and helping Christina into her seat, Eli said, "At last, an evening alone with my bride. We'd better hurry before someone decides they need us again!"

He climbed into his seat, took up the reins, and gently urged the horse forward. Just as he turned to speak, Christina said, "Eli, I forgot to mention—Seth stopped by last week when you were gone." Seth Bullock, the sheriff of Deadwood, was a close friend of Eli's. Eli had once been one of Seth's deputies and still lent a hand with law duties when needed.

"He said he wanted to talk to you about some horse thieves in the area," Christina continued. "Are there really horse thieves around here?"

Eli looked puzzled. "I hadn't heard anything about it," he replied. "When did Seth come by, and why did this just now come to mind?" he added with a slight grin, knowing Christina didn't like the potential danger that came with his occasional law work.

"Well, I thought he'd be back by now to see you. Since he hasn't come around again, maybe the problem has disappeared," Christina said, raising an eyebrow. "I know he's a good friend and he's helped us when we needed it, but law work isn't like hauling lumber. It's dangerous."

"Oh, you should've seen the splinter I got from that last load of lumber! Nearly took me out," Eli teased. Christina playfully rolled her eyes. "Just promise me you won't put yourself in harm's way. We have a ranch to pay for," she said.

They reached the Stagebarns and stopped by the benches near the creek to unpack their supper. But as Eli unloaded the basket, he noticed a rider approaching. "Looks like Henry," he said to Christina. "You go on down to the creek, and I'll be along shortly."

Henry trotted up and called out, "Hello, Christina! I won't keep him long!"

Christina looked back, smiling and waving as she continued down to the creek. Turning to Eli, Henry said, "Sorry to disturb you two, but I just heard of your return when I was in Spearfish. Sheriff Bullock caught me leaving Deadwood this morning and asked me to tell you he could use your help."

"I was just hearing about that myself," Eli replied, glancing toward Christina by the creek.

"Seems he's looking for someone," Henry said. "Does it have anything to do with your trip to Fort Pierre?"

"No, I think it's about some horse thieves. I'll check in with Seth tomorrow," Eli replied. "But my trip to Fort Pierre didn't go quite as planned. I found a few leads, though. Speaking of which, is the stone with my uncle's name still on display at Cashner Mercantile?"

"As far as I know," said Henry. "You heading back there to check on it?"

"Yes. I need to take another look," Eli said. Then, glancing back at the creek, he added, "But for now, I'd better get to my promised evening with Christina."

"Right," Henry chuckled. "I won't be the one to delay that! We'll catch up soon; you know I'm by here often enough." Henry tipped his hat and spurred his horse toward Deadwood. "Oh, and by the way," he called back, "Calamity Jane's in Deadwood again. I'm sure she'll be looking for you!"

Eli rolled his eyes and shouted back, "Thanks for the warning!" Grabbing the basket, he headed down to the creek to join Christina.

As he unpacked the basket, Christina said, "Seems everyone's looking for you these days."

"Maybe," Eli replied, "but you've got all of me now."

The rest of the evening was just as they'd planned—catching up and enjoying each other's company. Christina told Eli about the guests they'd had while he was away and mentioned a few improvements she wanted, like a way to signal guests from their rooms when the stage was ready. Eli promised to work on a solution. He shared the story of the DeLacompt family and the mysterious paper with Christina, explaining that it was the main reason he'd be heading back to Spearfish to examine the stone again and to explore the location that Louis Thoen found the stone. Christina offered her help in any way she could, though she gently reminded him to be cautious about setting high expectations.

She also expressed her usual concern about his work with Sheriff Bullock—a worry Eli knew was her way of showing care. They shared a beautiful evening filled with good conversation and laughter, particularly over the stories they'd inevitably hear when Calamity Jane caught up with them. It was dark by the time they returned to the Stagehouse and settled in for the night.

Chapter 4 – Old friends in Deadwood

Eli was almost finished with the Saturday morning chores when he noticed the stage coming up the driveway. He hurried inside to let Christina know. As he opened the door, the smell of freshly baked bread made his mouth water. He'd seen the dough rising on the counter when he left for chores and knew why Christina had been up so early.

"Christina! The stage is coming up the driveway!" he called.

He found her in the kitchen, pulling a pan of golden buns from the oven. Eli inhaled deeply, savoring the aroma as she brushed butter over the tops.

"I'm almost ready," Christina said without looking up. "These buns are for the guests. The bread will be ready soon, but that's for later."

"I'm almost ready to head out to see Seth in Deadwood," Eli replied. "Do you need anything before I go?"

"No, I think everything's set until you get back later today," Christina said with a quick smile. Eli gave her a kiss and stepped out to greet the guests, guiding them inside before returning to the barn to mount up for Deadwood.

The day was dreary, with fog lingering over the ridges to the south. Anticipating moisture from the clouds, Eli pulled his slicker from the back of his saddle and slipped it on.

By mid-morning, he reached the outskirts of Deadwood. A steady drizzle had continued throughout his ride, and the muddy streets of Deadwood bore the tracks of horses and wagons. He noticed the

Deadwood Street Railway parked in front of the Gem Saloon—a horse-drawn trolley system that had initially been the town's pride. Despite its "big city" sophistication, Eli noted it wasn't often used.

As he dismounted, Sheriff Bullock stepped out of his office. "I saw you coming, so I thought I'd act like I was busy," Bullock joked.

"And here I was, hoping to catch you napping at this time of day!" Eli shot back with a grin.

Bullock leaned against a hitching post. "I'd almost given up on you, but Henry stopped by to tell me you were back and planning to come by today."

"Seems your spies always know how to track me down, Seth," Eli replied. "I hear you have a project that could use an extra hand?"

Seth Bullock

Bullock nodded, and they headed back inside the small office, where jail cells lined the walls around Bullock's desk and down the hall.

Seth took his seat behind his desk, while Eli settled into a chair across from him, glancing at the cells.

"Looks like you had a busy Friday night," Eli remarked, eyeing the mostly full cells.

Seth nodded. "Most of them are still sleeping it off, so we shouldn't have too much trouble—though I could be wrong," he added, as a clang echoed from a cell. Someone had knocked over a pail and immediately began retching into it. Turning to the cell, Seth called, "Bill, you'd better hit that pail, and if I catch a whiff of that, you'll be here longer than you thought!"

Shaking his head, he turned back to Eli. "Anyway, back to business—I know you don't want to spend all day here. Last week, the Dixon ranch reported two gray mares missing from their pasture. They were spotted outside of Belle Fourche a couple of days later. I have a decent description of the cowboys who were seen with the mares, and I suspect they're still in the area. I don't want to send a big posse after them, as that might spook them before we can get close. Don Mette from the feed store is keeping an eye out since he delivers in that area. We'll check in with him once we reach Belle. If you're willing to lend a hand, that is?"

Eli thought of Christina's worried face as he quickly agreed, "Sure, when do we leave?"

"I know you haven't been home long, but I'd like to head out early tomorrow. If they're taking Sunday as a day of rest, it might make things easier for us."

Eli stood up. "I'll grab some supplies while I'm in town and head back home to catch up on a few things."

Seth followed him to the door. "One more thing, Eli. Jane showed up a few days ago. She hasn't spent any time in my cells yet, but I figure it's only a matter of time."

26

Eli rolled his eyes. "Henry warned me last night that she was looking for me. I'd better find her while I'm here; otherwise, she'll end up showing up at the house."

"Probably a good idea, "See you by 4 tomorrow morning." Seth replied

Eli nodded while mounting his horse and turned toward the hardware store. He cast a glance at the Gem Saloon with the unused Street Railway in front. Seth called after him, "If you're looking for Jane, she'll likely be at the Gem and if you are wondering if the Street Railway gets used much the answer is no!"

"You read my mind, my friend," Eli said.

Tying off his horse beside the Street Railway, Eli considered the abandoned trolley a waste of time and money, though at least it wasn't at his expense. As he entered the Gem, before his eyes even adjusted to the smoky dimly-lit room, he heard Jane's unmistakable voice. It had been a while since they'd seen each other—probably back when he'd recovered from smallpox and first met Christina. His thoughts drifted to his first encounter with Jane during the Newton Jenney expedition, when she'd posed as a bullwhacker named John. That was the first time Eli had believed such language and rough talk could come from a woman. Seeing her again, in rough shape, he was reminded of how she'd earned her name, Calamity Jane.

When she spotted him, her voice bellowed across the room. "I'll be damned! If it isn't pretty boy Eli, finally back in town! I heard you and the Mrs. have a new place of your own." She kept talking, never removing the cigar from her mouth. "I was about to come find you, but these fine gentlemen invited me for a game of cards."

Eli glanced around the table, noting that "fine gentlemen" might be a stretch, as the men looked like they'd been dusted off after days of hard digging.

"Jane, I figured I'd better find you first—for a lot of reasons," Eli replied. He could see that Jane looked worse than he remembered—not that she'd ever been a picture of health, but she looked even more haggard.

Jane gathered the few chips she had and excused herself in typical fashion. "You bastards have a nice day. I've got someone better to talk to!" The other players glared but returned to their game as Jane motioned for Eli to join her at another table.

Eli dusted off a chair and sat down as Jane plopped into the other seat, sending a cloud of dust across the table. "Jane, what brings you back to Deadwood?" he asked.

Jane reached into her buckskin jacket and pulled out an envelope that was surprisingly clean compared to the rest of her. "I wanted to see you, Eli. You're the only one I'd trust with this," she said, handing him the envelope. "I've had a hard life, and a lot of it's my own fault, but I've got my daughter Janey to think of. I need someone to make sure she gets what's hers."

Eli opened the envelope and began reading as Jane continued, "I've been doing all right on my ranch on Canyon Creek, though the local tribes leave me alone only because they think I'm possessed. I put on a good show, but lately, I can barely get up most days."

Eli set down the letter, realizing he'd dusted it by placing it on the table, then quickly picked it back up. "I'm sorry, Jane," he muttered.

"Sorry for what?" Jane scoffed. "I need Janey to remember me." Eli scanned the letter again, reading aloud:

"This is my last will, and I bequeath to my only heiress, my daughter Janey Hickok O'Neil, all my possessions: my ranch on Canyon Creek, my saddle, trunk of keepsakes, wedding ring, and brooch of gold with pearls."

Jane added, "Oh, and my horse, Satan. He's at the stables and will probably outlive me. He might bring Janey a little joy, as he did me."

Eli leaned forward. "I'll help you, Jane, but I don't even know where to start."

"I know. That's why I wanted to explain it to you myself," Jane replied. She waved to the bartender, demanding loudly, "What does it take to get a drink around here?"

The bartender set a glass of whiskey down in front of Eli, then another in front of Jane with a scowl, before walking off. Jane began explaining her story. "I've lived a life I'm not too proud of, but I'm not sure I'd change much—except for Janey and us being separated. I told you I met James Butler Hickok—Wild Bill, as you knew him—in Abilene, Kansas, in '70. It was love at first sight. Bill was the marshal, and I'd heard all the stories about his wild days. We got married that year, and he swore those days were behind him, that he wanted a life with me."

She continued, "Janey was born in '73, and that's when things took a turn. Bill had a run-in with some cowboys bent on killing him. In the gunfight, he was accused of shooting the Deputy Marshal, which got him relieved of his duties. That's when the drinking and gambling began. Not long after, he met Buffalo Bill Cody and joined his traveling show. He was restless. I thought he'd want us to come along, but instead, he just left us. I was devastated, and that's when I made the mistake I can't take back."

Jane sighed deeply. "I met a rich sea captain named James O'Neil, who took a liking to Janey. My selfishness took over when he said he'd like to raise her as his own. All I wanted was to find Bill, and that's what I set out to do. I followed Cody's Wild West Show, even joined in it. Bill and I drifted further apart. He told me he was going to try to find a cure for his failing eyesight, and then he left the show."

29

"Captain O'Neil took Janey back to England with him. I wrote to her whenever I could, and the captain sent me pictures. Janey's the spitting image of me at her age," she said, tears welling up in her eyes. "I just couldn't get over Bill. When I met you, Eli, I had just missed him in Cheyenne. Then, on the expedition, when we returned to Cheyenne, I ran into our old friend Charlie Utter. He told me he and Bill were headed to the Black Hills to seek their fortune in gold. Is Charlie still around?"

Eli looked down at his untouched glass. "Not long after he made Bill's headstone, I heard he'd headed back to Colorado. I haven't heard from him since."

Jane threw back another glass of whiskey, motioning to the bartender for a refill. "Charlie was a good cuss and a loyal friend to Bill. I added to his burdens by convincing him to let me tag along to the Black Hills. Bill wasn't happy to see me, but he eventually warmed up." She leaned in, giving Eli a wink as if to remind him that she and Bill had been lovers. "I told him about Janey. He acted indifferent, but I know he'd have wanted a good life for her."

Eli noticed the clock on the wall and began to move his chair back. He folded Jane's paper and slid it into his jacket pocket. "Jane, there's so much you've never shared. I'll do my best to honor your request with the will. How long are you staying in Deadwood?"

"Until they run out of whiskey—or I die. Maybe both!" Jane laughed.

Calamity Jane

Eli stood. "I need to get to the hardware store before it closes. You should come visit us at the ranch sometime. Christina would love to see you," he added, picturing Christina's cringing face at the thought of Jane's visit. But Jane was his friend, and he'd help her however he could.

Jane glanced at Eli's untouched whiskey and said, "That whiskey ain't gonna drink itself."

"It's all yours," he replied. Jane grabbed the glass. "I'd better get back to my game, and you'd better get back to the Mrs. Thanks for the talk, Eli. You've always been someone I could talk to." She was well past making a full sentence, and Eli wondered how she'd manage to get back to the card table, let alone play a hand. He gave her a hug and told her he'd see her soon, mentioning he'd be gone helping Sheriff Bullock for a few days.

As Eli left the Gem, he heard Jane bellowing at the other players as she stumbled back to the table, cussing them out all the while.

Eli had even more on his mind as he made his way to the hardware store. He needed to be ready to go with the Sheriff in the morning, and now Jane's issues weighed on him too. There'd be plenty to explain to

Christina, but he hoped his hardware purchase would help soften the not-so-good news.

Harris Franklin had come to Deadwood a few years ago, and Eli had met him several times when they'd both been building their homes—Harris in town and Eli at the Stagehouse. They'd swapped ideas and helped each other a few times. The Franklins had quickly made a small fortune in liquor sales on Deadwood's Main Street. Now president of the bank, Harris was also dabbling in ranching and mining ventures. His home had every luxury: central heating, hot and cold running water, electric lights, electric bells to summon servants, and even a telephone—an ideal of modern American life.

Eli had talked to Harris about the bell system and how helpful it would be when guests lingered too long upstairs while the stage waited. Too often, they claimed they hadn't heard the stage arrive, meaning Christina had to go up and herd them out. Harris had ordered the bell system from Chicago through the hardware store, and a month ago, Eli had placed an order too, which he hoped had arrived.

As Eli approached the store, he tried to think of anything else he might need but was mostly focused on the surprise he had planned for Christina. Best just to get his order and head out before something else delayed him!

A familiar voice greeted him from behind the counter. It was Sol Star, the store owner and Sheriff Bullock's business partner. "Hello, Eli! I saw you coming up the street, so I went ahead and grabbed your order from the back."

"Aw, Sol, you know I just come here to see you!" Eli joked. "But yes, that's what I'm here for. I want to get out of town before I get caught up in something else."

"I know the Sheriff needed you. Is there something else going on?" Sol asked.

"Yeah," Eli said. "I ran into Jane, so I'm sure you understand."

Sol chuckled. "Oh, yes, I heard she was looking for you. It's not like her to be quiet, and she doesn't look in good health."

Eli picked up his package, turning toward the door. "According to her, she doesn't think she has much time left."

Sol nodded thoughtfully. "She's never had an easy life, but there's a good person behind that rough exterior."

"I know, Sol. She did a lot for the town during the smallpox outbreak, and I could see how much she cared—she was also hurt by Bill. Keep an eye on her, if you would. I'll check in when the Sheriff and I return."

Sol nodded, and Eli said his goodbyes, making his way to the street to secure his package for the ride home.

Chapter 5 – The Sheriff's Mission

Eli arrived home just as the sun was setting behind Crow Peak. After untacking his horse and giving her some well-deserved grain, he was surprised by Christina at the barn door. Startled, Eli jumped back slightly, almost dropping the package he was holding.

"Christina, you scared me!" Eli exclaimed.

"Sorry, Eli," she said, laughing. "I didn't mean to startle you. I just saw you ride up and wanted to be the first to greet you—we have a full house tonight." Eli set down the package and reached out to embrace her.

"Well, you got me this time, Christina," he replied, chuckling as they shared a short kiss.

"Did you bring me something?" Christina asked playfully.

"I did, and I was going to surprise you with it, but you already caught me!" Eli replied, smiling. "Remember when I told you about the bell system the Franklins put in their house in Deadwood?"

"Yes, I remember," Christina replied. "You've told me about all the fancy things the Franklins have that we can't afford."

"Well, this will pay for itself by saving you the trouble of going upstairs to round up guests for the stage," Eli explained.

"What do you mean?" Christina asked, intrigued.

"When I get back from helping the Sheriff, I'm going to install this bell system." Eli opened the package. "When the stage arrives, you'll

34

be able to ring the bell upstairs again and again until the guests come down!"

"That sounds wonderful!" Christina said, a big grin spreading across her face.

"Seth will be here early tomorrow, so I'd better get to bed soon. Hope you'll join me?" Eli added, winking.

"I'll be there as soon as I check on my breakfast supplies for tomorrow," Christina replied.

A chill hung in the morning air as Eli saddled up Ginger. Sheriff Bullock should be arriving any moment, he thought, as he glanced out the barn window for any sign. He tightened his saddlebags and tied on his knapsack, just in case the trip took longer than expected. Christina had reminded him of the danger involved and urged him to be careful. He thought back to the close calls he'd had over the years with Seth, though things had always turned out well enough. Seth was a skilled negotiator, and Eli trusted that today's mission would go the same way.

Just then, the small barn door swung open, and Sheriff Bullock's bushy eyebrows and intense eyes appeared in the doorway. "Morning, Eli," Seth said in his low, gravelly voice. "Didn't mean to startle you."

Eli, visibly surprised, replied, "I just checked outside and didn't see anyone—guess you caught me off guard."

Seth made his way to the main barn door, opening it as he spoke. "I'm sure you're wide awake now, and ready for this little outing?"

Eli led his packed horse out of the barn, following Seth. "So you say this is just a 'little' outing? Christina keeps reminding me that dealing with criminals isn't exactly the same as a day spent fencing," he joked.

"True," Seth replied, "but I don't think this one's going to get too messy."

"Good," Eli said, mounting his horse. "So, what's our mission again?"

"We'll talk on the way," Seth said, swinging onto his horse. "I'd rather this didn't turn into a full day's ride if we can avoid it."

With that, the two men trotted down the driveway, heading northwest toward Spearfish. As they rode, Seth explained that he'd received word about a horse thief who'd been working with a group of cowboys returning from a cattle drive to Medora, North Dakota. Their plan was to intercept the group and identify the thief. Eli questioned how they'd know which one was the thief among the cowboys.

Seth chuckled. "We'll get them in a spot where we can question them. I've got a pretty good idea of his appearance."

"Let me guess," Eli said dryly. "Wide-brimmed hat, worn shirt, cowboy vest and waistcoat, leather chaps, tall boots with spurs, and an oversized handkerchief around his neck?"

Seth grinned. "Well, this one also wears spectacles and is rough-shaven."

"That does narrow it down," Eli replied with a smirk.

By noon, they'd reached the Belle Fourche River and spotted a campfire in the distance. The day had warmed considerably, and both men felt the sun's heat after the hard ride. Seth pulled back on the reins, dismounted, and pulled a telescope from his saddlebag to scan the camp.

"See anything?" Eli asked.

"Yeah," Seth replied. "There are a few cowboys around the fire, and a couple others off to the side—could be on lookout. We'd better be cautious from here on out." He collapsed the telescope, put it back in his saddlebag, and the two men unstrapped their rifles from their saddles.

As they rode forward, they encountered a man on horseback who'd just crossed the Belle. Eli noticed that the man matched Seth's description, right down to the spectacles. Seth stopped, drew his gun, and called out in a commanding voice, "Hold it right there! My name is Sheriff Bullock, and this here is my deputy. We're looking for a wanted man, so I'll need you to identify yourself!"

The stranger raised his hands. "Easy there, Sheriff," he replied calmly. "I'm just out here with my men from Medora, searching the Belle this morning."

Seth kept his gun steady, eyeing the man closely. Eli held his rifle, ready to back Seth up. The stranger continued, "I'll dismount and show you I'm unarmed, so we can sort this out—if that's all right with you?"

The man dismounted, keeping his hands raised as he opened his fringed vest to reveal he was unarmed. Seth and Eli held their firearms steady, still wary, as the man looked at Seth and said, "I'd never make a move on someone with a stare like yours, Sheriff."

Eli smiled slightly, recognizing the stranger's apt description of Seth. "My name is Teddy Roosevelt," the man continued, "and I'm the Sheriff and a landowner near Medora, North Dakota. If you want, my deputy here can check my saddlebag—I've got my badge and other papers in there."

Seth gave Eli a nod, and Eli dismounted to check the saddlebag, finding a badge and papers about the Elk Horn Ranch near Medora. He glanced at Seth. "Seems he's telling the truth."

Roosevelt added, "I didn't mean anything by calling you 'ministerial,' Sheriff, but I'd appreciate it if you let me put my hands down now."

Seth finally holstered his gun. "You can put your hands down, but we'll have more questions for you."

Roosevelt relaxed, lowering his hands. "I understand you're looking for a horse thief, and it just so happens that we're searching for one too—he's made off with some of my horses and headed for Wyoming to sell them."

"So, he stole them from you?" Eli asked.

"Yes," Roosevelt replied. Seth shot Eli a look, signaling him to hold back. After reading Roosevelt's papers, Seth returned his gun to its holster.

"All right, Mr. Roosevelt, your story checks out," Seth said, though his intense gaze stayed fixed on Roosevelt. "We'll check in with your men back at camp to confirm it."

They rode into the camp together, where three cowboys were heating up beans by the fire. Recognizing Roosevelt, they nodded and relaxed a little. Sheriff Bullock spoke up. "Good afternoon. I'm Sheriff Bullock, and I'm here with my deputy to investigate a horse thief in this area. Your friend here claims to be part of your group. Can you confirm this?"

One of the cowboys, Tom Crandell, spoke up. "Sheriff, my name's Tom Crandell. Mr. Roosevelt deputized us to help find the thief—so we're all working for him." He gestured to the others around the campfire.

"Then I'll need to speak with all of you," Seth replied, his tone still firm. Just then, another cowboy rode up, causing Seth to draw his gun. Roosevelt quickly stepped in front of him.

"He's one of mine, Sheriff," Roosevelt said. Seth lowered his gun and asked, "Any more out there?"

Tom nodded toward the ridge across the river. "Whitey's out there on lookout. He's not likely to come down, though."

"Why not?" Seth asked.

Roosevelt answered, "Whitey's been with us since last year. He's a drifter, and he prefers his own company. He's no thief, though."

"I'd still like to speak to him," Seth replied, mounting his horse again. "Eli, stay here and get everyone's names. I'll go meet this, Whitey."

As Seth rode off, Roosevelt turned to Eli and commented, "Sheriff Bullock's a formidable fellow, with a look like a hawk. But if he doesn't ease up a bit, I fear he'll explode!"

Eli chuckled. "That sounds about right. He's been like that since I've known him."

"I think I'm going to like him," Roosevelt replied with a grin.

Eli, Roosevelt, and the cowboys continued their conversation, discussing the stolen horses and the ongoing search for the thief.

Teddy Roosevelt

When the Sheriff returned, they all shared a few laughs about the day's unexpected meeting. Roosevelt, who insisted they call him "Teddy" from now on, decided he and his men would stay on the trail of the horse thief and report to Sheriff Bullock if they found any leads. This meant that Eli and Seth could head back and, hopefully, make it home before nightfall.

On the ride back, Eli and Seth discussed the day's events, and Eli had a chance to ask Seth how he'd known that Teddy wasn't the horse thief.

"I usually get a sense once I look someone in the eye," Seth explained. "When I ask a direct question—like where they've come from—and they look away or hesitate, I know there's more to find. But Mr. Roosevelt—Teddy—didn't flinch at all. That's when I figured we weren't in for trouble, though I wasn't about to let them know that right away."

Eli thought to himself, *yes, Seth certainly has that death stare down. Even I can never tell what his next move will be.*

Eli then asked, "And what did you make of his cowboy, Whitey? You didn't say much, just that you 'found him.'"

Seth looked off into the distance as they rode along, then turned back to Eli. "I'm still thinking that over. I don't believe he's involved in any theft, and I believe Teddy's right about him not liking company. There's a story behind that big bushy white beard and hair of his—the reason they call him Whitey. When I asked where he was from, all he said was, 'Not from these parts.' I could see he didn't want to give more, so I let it go. At his age, I don't think he's looking to start trouble."

"Fair assumption," Eli replied.

The two made a quick stop for supper in Spearfish before reaching the Kind Ranch at dusk. Christina was waiting in the barn doorway as they rode up, greeting Eli with a warm kiss as he dismounted. Seth said his goodbyes, and Christina thanked him for bringing Eli back safely. Eli joked that perhaps he'd been the one keeping Seth safe, prompting a rare smile from the Sheriff.

Seth turned, gave a casual wave, and headed down the lane toward Deadwood. Eli and Christina stayed up for a while, sharing stories of their day and agreeing to spend time on their own projects in the coming days.

Chapter 6 – Home on the Ranch

The Kind ranch buzzed with activity, as Eli worked to tackle the backlog of projects that had piled up during his absence. He began with the buzzer system he'd promised Christina. With the stage guests picked up, he had the house to himself, and before long, the new "buzz" resonated throughout. Now, when guests lingered upstairs while the stage waited, Christina wouldn't have to climb the stairs to hurry them along. Eli installed the button by the door, making it easy to check for the stage and sound the buzzer. Christina remarked that the sound would take some getting used to, but it was a welcome change.

With the main task checked off, Eli headed to the Anderson ranch to help with fencing along the "milk road." The milk road was the main route connecting the Kind ranch to Deadwood, running through Anderson land. Eli knew the road well, having traveled it almost daily during his courtship of Christina, and now he used it to lend a hand to his in-laws. James and Catherine Anderson constantly worked to improve their ranch, and Eli often pitched in, even taking the 10-mile trip himself to sell Anderson milk in Deadwood.

James wanted better grazing control for his cattle, so they'd been working to fence off the milk road into two pastures. The project had been low priority, but with the frost of winter approaching, it was time to finish before the ground made post-setting impossible.

As Eli rounded a bend in the milk road, he saw James hard at work, pulling rocks from a freshly dug hole.

"Good afternoon, Eli. I take it you've been catching up on your chores?" James greeted him with a grunt as he rolled another rock aside.

"Yes," Eli replied. "I installed that buzzer system I told you about."

"That should make my daughter happy," James said, prying another rock loose with a grunt.

Eli dismounted and joined him, helping to roll the rock out of the way. "You never know what you'll hit or miss in this stretch of land," Eli mused.

The fence, forming a lane along the milk road, was nearly complete. Eli estimated they had about ten posts left to set, which meant they'd soon need to cut more timber from the ranch's stand of pitch pines. James had taught Eli a technique passed down from his Dutch ancestors: cutting the top third of a ponderosa pine and allowing the bottom two-thirds to "pitch out" for a year. The resulting sticky wood created durable posts that lasted for decades.

The pair worked methodically, digging holes and setting posts with precision. As they labored, conversation turned to expanding the dairy herd, the challenges of grazing livestock, and Eli's recent trips to Fort Pierre and Deadwood. James listened as Eli shared his progress—or lack thereof—in solving the mystery of his uncle Ezra's disappearance. James was supportive, though pragmatic, about Eli's quest.

As they set the final post of the day, James leaned on his shovel and said, "Eli, have you heard the story of Levi Blizzard?"

"No, I haven't," Eli replied, intrigued.

James explained, "He was found dead in the blizzard of '76 near Lookout Mountain. No one knew his real name, but he was wearing Levi's, so that's what folks called him—Levi Blizzard."

Eli's eyes lit up. "I can't believe I've never heard of this before!"

James grinned. "I figured that'd get your attention. He's buried at Rose Hill Cemetery in Spearfish, but that's all I know."

Eli fell silent, lost in thought. James added, "I hate to disappoint you, but I don't think Levi Blizzard is your missing uncle. That stone Louis Thoen found with your uncle's name—if there was a connection, Louis would've uncovered it by now. Still, you might want to talk to him."

Shaking off his thoughts, Eli nodded. "You're probably right, but I can't help feeling like I'm so close to figuring it all out."

James clapped him on the back. "Pack it up for today. I need to get home to milk, and we're nearly out of posts anyway. I'll see you tomorrow—after you've talked to Louis," he added with a knowing smile.

That evening, Eli took his time finishing chores, his mind preoccupied with Levi Blizzard. When he finally stepped into the Stagehouse, Christina immediately noticed his troubled expression.

"What's on your mind, Eli?" she asked.

He sighed. "It's like you and your father have this way of knowing things before I do."

"What do you mean?" Christina asked, puzzled.

44

Eli launched into the story James had told him about Levi Blizzard. Christina listened intently, then gestured for him to sit at the kitchen table.

"Let's figure this out," she said, pulling up a chair. "But I have never heard of this name before."

"The fact that you've never heard of Levi Blizzard gives me a little hope that this is nothing," Eli admitted. "But I can't help wondering why your father never mentioned it before, knowing how much I've been searching for Ezra."

"Do you think my father kept it from you on purpose?" Christina asked.

Eli hesitated. "I don't know. But he doesn't think there's a connection, and he told me I should talk to Louis Thoen."

Christina leaned forward, cupping Eli's face in her hands. "And I'm sure you will," she said with a smile, kissing his forehead.

Eli chuckled. "That's exactly what your father said."

"Well, we both know you better than you know yourself," she teased, turning to the stove. "Now, make a list of supplies to pick up in Spearfish tomorrow while you're visiting Louis. Oh, and by the way, Sheriff Bullock stopped by. He wants you to come to Deadwood on Saturday—your new friend Teddy Roosevelt will be in town."

"New friend?" Eli grinned. "Is someone jealous of my social circle?"

"That depends," Christina replied playfully. "Someone has to keep this place running while you're off making friends!"

45

Chapter 7 – Looking for Answers

The next morning, Eli was up early, finishing his chores and preparing for a trip to Spearfish. His saddlebag contained a supply list and, more importantly, a set of burning questions for Louis Thoen. Within minutes of leaving the ranch, Eli could see the south side of Lookout Mountain, where the Thoen brothers worked their sandstone quarry. It was quiet today, likely meaning Louis was tending to his bees and orchard at his homestead below the mountain.

As Eli approached the orchard, he noticed smoke rising from Louis's bee smoker, used to calm the hives. Sure enough, Louis was busy extracting honeycombs when Eli dismounted his horse. Spotting him, Louis set down the smoker and walked over to greet him.

"Hello, Eli. What brings you to my honey orchard?"

"It should be for the honey and the orchard," Eli chuckled, "but I've got a question for you. I can see you're busy getting ready for winter, so I'll get right to the point. Have you heard the story of Levi Blizzard?"

Louis nodded thoughtfully. "Oh yes, I know it well. I thought the same thing I'm guessing you're about to ask—whether Levi could be your uncle from the Thoen Stone. When I first learned about Levi, I was sure he had to be Ezra or one of the others. But after some investigation, I ruled it out. Levi was too young to have been part of that group. There was also talk he worked at the Tinton mine, which was primarily staffed by colored folk, so I had to set the connection aside. However, Henry Frawley might know more about his burial, as he had a hand in securing the location for the burial."

"No need to trouble him," Eli replied. "I can tell you want answers as much as I do. I'll keep searching elsewhere. I'd better let you get back to work—your bees are starting to notice this stranger!" He ducked away from a buzzing bee, making Louis laugh.

"Before you go," Louis said, reaching into a nearby crate, "take this." He handed Eli a jar of honey. "I know it's not the story you wanted, but at least you won't leave empty-handed."

"Thanks, Louis," Eli replied, slipping the jar into his saddlebag. "I'll make a quick stop at Cashner's for supplies, and I'd like to make another rubbing of the Thoen Stone—it's getting a bit worn."

"It's still there," Louis confirmed. "Good luck, Eli. Don't give up."

"I won't, and neither should you," Eli called back as he rode away.

Louis Thoen

Eli sped through his errands at Cashner Hardware, picking up supplies with the help of John Cashner, who quickly deduced that Eli was eager to get back to work. Eli made it home in time to help James finish the fence along the Milk Road. Reluctantly, he shared the disappointing news about Levi Blizzard. James shrugged it off but offered encouraging words to keep Eli's resolve strong.

By Saturday, the work at the ranch was caught up enough for Eli to take Christina with him to Deadwood to meet Teddy Roosevelt. Christina's mother, Catherine, offered to manage the Stagehouse so Christina could go along. As Eli helped her into the buggy, she teased, "You know this means I'll owe her a favor—probably making cream and butter for her later."

Eli smiled knowingly. "You don't seem to mind too much."

Arriving in Deadwood around mid-afternoon, they left their buggy at the Montana Corral Stables and made their way to Sheriff Bullock's office in the Bullock Hotel. The building was impressive, decorated in "Italianate" and Victorian style, with a grand lobby and offices on the first floor. They were greeted by Sol Star, the mayor and Seth's business partner, who led them to the office where Seth and Teddy awaited.

"Ah, Eli," Seth greeted them with a wave. "I see you brought your lovely bride to grace our humble town."

"Yes, and I'd like to introduce Christina to Mr. Roosevelt," Eli said.

Teddy stood, moving quickly to shake Christina's hand, then gallantly kissed it. "The pleasure is mine, Christina. And please, call me Teddy. I can see Eli is a lucky man."

"Thank you, Teddy. That's very kind of you," Christina replied, blushing.

Seth then clapped his hands together. "Alright, folks. I hate to rush, but Teddy has a speech to give down the street. Let's head out."

As they walked, Christina whispered to Eli, "You didn't tell me he was a preacher."

Eli chuckled softly. "I didn't know either."

The crowd outside the Gem Saloon was sizable, gathered around a makeshift podium of wooden crates stacked atop what appeared to be caskets. Teddy launched into an impassioned speech, urging citizens to "get in the arena" and extolling the virtues of the Republican Party.

Eli leaned toward Christina. "So, not a preacher. A politician."

Christina leered. "Same energy."

As the speech continued, Eli spotted Henry Frawley in the crowd. Grabbing Christina's hand, he whispered, "I need to ask Henry something. Let's move closer."

After the speech, Eli caught Henry's attention. "I've got a question for you about Levi Blizzard."

Henry nodded knowingly. "Ah, Levi. I see where you're headed. But I'll save you the trouble—he was too young to be anyone from the Thoen Stone. The man I helped bury was a colored fellow, likely working in the mines, and he couldn't have been connected to your uncle. I wish I had better news for you."

Eli sighed. "Thanks, Henry. I needed to hear it from you directly."

The evening culminated in a lively dinner with many of Deadwood's notable figures, including Mayor Sol Star, Al Swearengen, W.E. Adams and Thomas Grier. Teddy charmed the room with his thoughts on conservation and ranching, sparking spirited conversations. Later, Seth invited Eli and Christina to the Bullock Hotel, where the group continued their discussions into the night.

As they rode home in the quiet darkness, Christina rested her head on Eli's shoulder. He smiled, knowing how much he appreciated her presence—not just today, but in his life.

Chapter 8 – Transforming the Black Hills

The Black Hills, especially around Deadwood, underwent such rapid transformation that it was often difficult for residents to keep up with the shifting land, people, and government actions. The early gold rush had slowed as placer mining along the streams gave way to hard rock mining, with prospectors tracing the creek leads back to the veins deep beneath the earth.

However, one of the most significant changes in the region came with the acquisition of the Manuel Brothers' claim by businessman and California Senator George Hearst. He established the Homestake Mine in Lead, marking the beginning of an era that would forever alter the Black Hills. Yet, this new phase came with its own set of challenges.

As an underground mine, Homestake caused the very ground beneath Lead to sink, necessitating the relocation of several buildings in the city. Another controversy arose over the mine's aggressive timber harvesting. Operating its own lumber mills, Homestake had already harvested enough timber to build more than 200,000 homes— but instead of constructing houses, the wood was primarily used to shore up the mine's underground tunnels.

This sparked sharp divisions among the people of the Black Hills. Some viewed the timber harvest as essential for keeping the mine operational and for thinning the forest—a crucial concern after the destructive Deadwood fires. Others, however, argued that the forest should be managed more responsibly, and that Homestake should pay for what it had taken from public lands.

Seth Bullock played a pivotal role in securing federal backing for better forest management. With support from conservationists like Gifford Pinchot and Theodore Roosevelt, Bullock helped push for the first-ever timber sale on Forest Reserve land. The buyer? Homestake Gold Mine. This groundbreaking sale near Nemo set a precedent for future forest conservation efforts in the region.

Despite these setbacks, Homestake remained one of the most influential companies in the area, driving modernization and transforming the Black Hills. It was more than just a prolific gold producer; it acted as a catalyst for change, turning Lead and its surroundings into a thriving hub of industry and innovation.

One of the mine's most notable contributions was the introduction of electricity. Homestake became the first mine in the United States to use electric power, as early as the 1880s. The company also established hydroelectric plants, such as the one on Spearfish Creek, to supply reliable power not only for the mine but for the surrounding towns as well. This initiative brought electric lighting to Lead and Deadwood long before rural America had access to such modern infrastructure.

In addition to electricity, the mine played a key role in improving sanitation and public health. Recognizing the importance of a healthy workforce, Homestake invested in water and sewer systems that provided clean water and reduced disease outbreaks. These improvements helped contribute to longer life expectancy and a higher quality of life for the people of the Black Hills, ensuring the well-being of miners and their families. As part of its commitment to health, Homestake also established one of the first corporate healthcare systems in the West, founding the Homestake Hospital and employing company doctors to care for the community.

The economic success of Homestake also attracted major railroad companies, which expanded their networks into the area. This allowed the mine to import supplies, equipment, and workers while exporting gold. The railroads opened up the Black Hills to national markets, further connecting the region to the broader economic landscape. The prosperity brought by the mine also spurred the development of educational institutions, including the South Dakota School of Mines & Technology.

Homestake's influence reached into nearly every aspect of daily life in the Black Hills. The company constructed housing for its workers, with homes featuring modern amenities such as indoor plumbing and heating.

Homestake Mine

Chapter 9 - Changes at the Kind Ranch

The Kind Ranch was evolving as well. Eli had entered a partnership with Henry Frawley on a land deal that expanded the ranch significantly. Over time, twenty original homesteads became part of the Kind Ranch. Many of these properties were obtained by Frawley, a skilled land lawyer, who took advantage of provisions in the Homestead Act.

The Homestead Act allowed any adult citizen, or intended citizen, who had never taken up arms against the U.S. government to claim 160 acres of surveyed government land. The requirement was that the claimant had to live on and "improve" the land by cultivating it. However, not all homesteaders were able to meet these requirements. When they struggled, Frawley offered them money to buy out their claims rather than letting the land revert to the government. Some saw this as a fair business deal—others viewed it as exploiting struggling settlers.

Regardless, the strategy worked. The ranch eventually exceeded 5,000 acres, making it necessary to divide the land into four sections: Upper, Middle, Lower, and East.

The East Ranch, also known as the Billy Grant Ranch, was a later and unexpected addition. Billy Grant had worked for Eli while also building his own ranch and raising his family. One day, on a routine supply trip to Spearfish, Billy never made it home. His team of horses and wagon arrived back at the ranch without him, causing panic among his family. It was later discovered that Billy had been struck by lightning on the way home and killed instantly. His sudden death ended his ranching enterprise, and his family ultimately sold their land to Eli.

With the added land and cattle, running the ranch required more than just family labor. Henry remained a silent partner, while Eli and four hired men from Spearfish expanded the Lower Ranch, constructing a granary with an elevator, a barn, and cattle shed.

Meanwhile, the completion of the railroad to Deadwood marked the end of the stagecoach era. The old stage barns were converted into calving sheds, and the once-bustling Stagehouse was no longer needed for overnight guests. However, Christina, always a gracious host, continued welcoming visitors to the ranch even as she took on more responsibilities in its daily operations.

The arrival of the railroad also brought improved communication. A telephone line was installed in the Kind Stagehouse, allowing Christina to call her mother at the Anderson Ranch with just a crank of the phone—eliminating the need for a 20-minute ride. She also formed a friendship with Kate, the operator in Spearfish, and found that chatting with her became a pastime for many women in the area. Eli, however, remained skeptical of the new technology. He saw the phone as an open invitation for more people to reach him, making it even harder for him to say no to anyone who needed help.

The biggest change to the Kind Ranch was the arrival of the newest Kind—Daniel Ezra Kind, the son of Eli and Christina. Just when they thought parenting meant dealing with the likes of Calamity Jane and the rowdy stagehouse guests, they were now raising a son.

From an early age, Daniel became an integral part of ranch life, helping with daily chores and working with the ever-expanding cattle herd. He had a special bond with Buster, the horse he raised from a colt. It was said that Daniel and Buster could read each other's minds, expertly cutting out any cow or calf from the herd. Eli and Christina couldn't have been prouder.

Daniel was now in seventh grade, one of the luckier students in the Centennial Valley, as his walk to school was only to the end of the driveway from the Kind Stagehouse. He had grown up hearing the story of his uncle Ezra from his father and eagerly shared it with his classmates and teacher, Mrs. Jillian Merager.

Ever since the discovery of the Thoen Stone, displayed at Cashner's Hardware Store, the local community had been abuzz with theories about what had happened to Ezra and his companions. Jillian Merager, who lived in Whitewood and was married to Kurtis Merager, the local sawmill owner, had heard the story through Daniel. Though she assumed her husband rarely paid attention to school gossip, she was stunned when he asked her if there had been any new developments in the search for Ezra Kind.

Intrigued, Jillian pressed Kurtis for details, and what he revealed left her speechless.

While delivering lumber to a ranch near Ludlow, the rancher, Albert Fenny, had shown Kurtis a cave with carvings in the hills near his property. One of the inscriptions, Kurtis claimed, looked remarkably similar to the writing on the Thoen Stone. After seeing the stone on display at Cashner's, he was convinced the cave's etchings were made by the same hand.

Jillian immediately relayed this discovery to Daniel, who in turn told Eli. At first, Eli dismissed it as just another dead-end lead. However, since he needed lumber, he decided to visit Kurtis and hear the story firsthand.

Chapter 10- A New Clue

When Eli arrived at the sawmill, he found Kurtis sharpening the big saw. "Hello, Kurtis. I need a couple of things from you—twelve rough-cut 2x10s and the story my boy has been telling me about this cave you found."

Kurtis looked up and smirked. "I wondered if you were going to come by. Not so much for the lumber, but to hear what I found. Not that I don't want you finishing your corrals—I've got all the 2x10s you need and more!"

Eli chuckled. "I figured the lumber was the easy part. It's just… I've been chasing my family's story for so long that I don't jump as fast as I used to."

"That's because you're old," Kurtis teased.

Eli laughed. "Yeah, that's it. Now, tell me what you know before I forget."

Inside the sawmill office, Kurtis described his encounter with Albert Fenny and the cave near Ludlow. He detailed the animal drawings and names carved into the rock, including one inscription that seemed freshly etched—eerily similar to the writing on the Thoen Stone.

Eli was skeptical but intrigued. Kurtis offered to take him to the site that Saturday, as he had another lumber delivery to Albert's ranch. Eli agreed and asked if Daniel could join them. Kurtis had no objections, and the plan was set.

Back home, Eli shared the news with Christina and Daniel. Daniel was thrilled, but Christina was hesitant.

"I just don't want to see you disappointed again," she admitted.

"I know," Eli replied. "But Kurtis seems pretty sure, and he's taking us straight there. Besides, it'll be a good trip for Daniel—this is the same area I explored during the expedition."

Saturday morning arrived with fog and cool temperatures, but Eli reassured Daniel that the fog would burn off soon. As they traveled north in the wagon full of lumber, Daniel peppered Kurtis with questions.

"What's all this lumber for?"

"It's a new ranch," Kurtis explained. "Albert built his house and barn right away, but now he's working on outbuildings, corrals, and a well house."

As the fog lifted, Eli recognized familiar landmarks from his 1874 expedition with Custer. He explained to Daniel that the landscape had looked much different back then, as wildfires had burned much of the area during their journey. Initially, they believed the Lakota had set the fires to prevent the soldiers' horses from grazing on their return trip. However, it was later revealed that careless campfires from the expedition itself were likely the cause.

When they arrived at Albert Fenny's ranch, they unloaded the wagon and prepared for the trek to the cave.

As they climbed the steep hill, Albert pointed to drawings on the rock face.

"Look up there," Daniel said excitedly. "It looks like an animal!"

"That's just the start," Albert explained. "The drawings go all the way up to the cave."

As they approached, Eli's excitement grew. He spotted a name with the date '74' carved into the rock.

"That's Major Tilford," Eli exclaimed. "He was on the cave exploration during our expedition!"

Then, inside the cave, Eli found exactly what Kurtis had described—etchings that matched the writing on the Thoen Stone.

Running his fingers across the etched letters, Eli whispered, "This has to be Ezra."

Now, more questions flooded his mind.

Where had Ezra gone?

How had he ended up here?

And most importantly—was he still alive?

Chapter 11 – More Clues

It was late when Eli and Daniel finally arrived home. Though Daniel was eager to tell his mother about what they had found, she convinced him that it could wait till morning.

Daniel could barely sit still at the table, talking so fast that he hardly had time to chew his food. In his excitement, it was as if they had solved the family mystery and brought home Ezra himself.

Eli let him talk but eventually reminded him, "Son, we need to prepare ourselves for the possibility that Ezra may not be alive. We may have only found the last place he lived."

"I bet the Indians got him, just like Mr. Fenny said," Daniel quipped.

"Daniel! That is not a respectful way to talk," Christina scolded.

Eli sighed. "Unfortunately, that may have happened, but we can't be sure."

"Yes, but that's not how we should be telling the story," Christina added. "Until we know what really happened, we should be careful with our words."

Daniel nodded and quickly changed the subject. "It was a great trip anyway. Thanks for taking me along, Dad. I learned a lot."

"I'm glad it worked out for you to come. And I'm glad you enjoyed it," Eli said. "Now, let's help your mother with the dishes and get our chores done. We have another engagement today."

"What engagement?" Daniel asked.

"We're all going to Deadwood to see Mr. Roosevelt present an award to Sheriff Bullock," Christina chimed in.

Daniel didn't say anything, but the look on his face made it clear—he wasn't exactly thrilled. Mr. Roosevelt's speeches tended to be long-winded, especially for a teenage boy.

Eli leaned in and whispered in Daniel's ear, "Who's to say we don't run into some buggy trouble along the way and happen to get there a little late?"

Daniel looked up at his father, catching the wink and smile before Eli bundled up to head outside.

Eli instructed Daniel to get the buggy ready while he tended to the animals. It was a crisp late-fall day, so he also told Daniel to pack some blankets—the ride home after dark was sure to be cold.

The journey to Deadwood was brisk but not unbearable. The last hints of autumn clung to the trees, though most of the leaves had already been stripped by the wind, leaving only the dark green pines as a stark contrast.

As promised, Eli made sure they arrived late—by the time they reached the Bullock Hotel, Roosevelt was already deep into his speech. The hotel lobby was packed, and Teddy stood on the stairway, addressing the crowd with his usual booming enthusiasm.

Slipping in behind Henry Frawley, Eli leaned in and whispered, "Did we miss anything important?"

"Well," Henry replied, "I don't think Seth will be our sheriff much longer. Teddy's got bigger plans for him."

"Like what?" Eli asked.

"Sounds like he's so impressed with Seth's work on the timber sales and conservation efforts that he wants him to be some kind of Forest Supervisor—helping to establish National Parks, whatever that is."

Eli frowned. "I know Teddy and Seth have been close ever since we met him on the Belle River, but I hate to think he'd leave Deadwood."

"I think Seth will do what Teddy asks," Henry said. "But he's got a ranch near the Belle now, and he's helped build up the town of Belle Fourche. I doubt he'll stay away from this area for long."

Eli nodded in agreement. "Yeah, I knew he was getting into ranching, and with Teddy's sons coming out here to learn the ranch life, I'd be surprised if Seth moved too far from the Hills."

At that moment, Teddy spotted Eli in the crowd.

"I see Mr. Kind has arrived to help us honor our good friend!" Teddy called out, his voice booming over the crowd. "And no, I am not stealing Seth away from your fine community—I just happen to know when good men are needed for great things! You might be next, Eli!"

Seth and Teddy

Eli smiled and gave a polite nod. He wasn't sure he needed another adventure in his life.

Teddy was just wrapping up—to the relief of Daniel, who was now eyeing a nearby window ledge for a place to sit—when he ended his speech with one of his famous quips:

"If you simply speak softly, the other man will bully you. If you leave your stick at home, you will find the other man did not. If you carry the stick only and forget to speak softly, in nine cases out of ten, the other man will have a bigger stick."

Eli and most of the crowd understood the wisdom in Teddy's words, while the rest simply applauded, impressed by his delivery. The room filled with cheers, and as the crowd began filing out, Eli took

Christina's hand and motioned for Daniel to follow—they had a personal congratulation to give Seth.

When they reached him, Seth was still surrounded by well-wishers. He caught Eli's eye and motioned for him to follow Teddy upstairs to the suite, a custom they had developed over the years at the Bullock Hotel.

The Bullock Hotel

Chapter 12 - Story Time with Uncle Teddy

B y the time the Kinds reached the second floor, Teddy was already waving them inside.

"Come on in!" he bellowed. "It's been too long since I've seen you all! Surely you have a story for Uncle Teddy—or maybe I have one for you!"

This was Daniel's favorite part of these visits. He wasn't a fan of speeches, but story time with "Uncle Teddy" was legendary. The hunting tales, war stories, and cowboy adventures had captivated him since he was little.

"I do have a story for you, Uncle Teddy!" Daniel blurted out, settling into a chair next to Roosevelt.

"Well, do tell!" Teddy said, beaming.

As Daniel excitedly recounted their discovery in the cave, Teddy sat forward in his seat, listening intently.

When Daniel finished, Teddy turned to Eli. "You called these the Ludlow Caves, correct?"

Eli nodded. "Yes, Major Ludlow named them when we passed through during the 1874 Expedition."

"So, I assume they're near the town of Ludlow?" Teddy pressed.

"The caves themselves are a bit farther north," Eli clarified.

Teddy thought for a moment, stroking his chin. "I know you've spent years chasing leads on Ezra—and I don't want to send you on another wild goose chase—but I just remembered something."

Eli and Christina exchanged glances.

Teddy leaned in. "About five years ago, we were in that area—my ranch hands called it Cave Hills. One of my men, Will, went out searching for a stray when he returned to camp with the cow and a stranger."

Eli's brow furrowed.

Teddy continued, "Will told me the man was looking for work. I needed hands, so I hired him. He called himself Whitey, and by God, he sure was—white hair, bushy white beard.

Eli's heart started pounding. Was this the same story he was told about the mysterious cave man the Indians talked about?

Teddy went on, "I never asked him much about his past, and to think of it now, he never talked much to the other ranch hands. He kept to himself—but he was invaluable when it came to treating sick livestock and injured men. In fact, he helped patch me up a few times while we were chasing down boat thieves."

Teddy suddenly grinned. "Which reminds me—that's a story worth telling," he said, turning toward Daniel, who perked right up, eager to listen.

Seth, who had been quietly sitting at the back of the room, suddenly stood and spoke. "Hold on, Teddy, you said Whitey was found by your ranch hand about five years ago? Wasn't he with you when we first met?"

Teddy paused, deep in thought. "I believe you're right."

"I know I am," Seth quipped. "I remember the white bushy beard and those blue eyes poking through all that hair. Does he still work for you?"

"Yes, he does," Teddy replied. "I don't let good men go from my ranch, and he's proven his worth. Like I said, he patched me up well after my tangle with the boat thieves. He claimed I had frostbite—I said it was just a nibble."

Teddy launched into the story of his pursuit and capture of the boat thieves in the Badlands, but Eli barely heard him.

Could Whitey have been Ezra?
Was he still alive?

Eli fought the urge to ask more questions and caught up with Teddy's story just as he was describing the boat.

"We had brought out a clinker-built boat, especially to ferry ourselves over the river when it was high, and were keeping our ponies on the opposite side. This boat had already proved very useful and now came in handier than ever, as without it, we could take no care of our horses. We kept it on the bank, tied to a tree, and every day we would carry it or slide it across the ice bank, usually with not a little tumbling and scrambling on our part, lower it gently into the swift current, pole it across to the ice on the farther bank, and then drag it over that..."

"One morning, before breakfast, one of my men came back to the house with startling news—our boat was gone. Stolen. He brought back the end of the rope, which had clearly been cut with a sharp knife. He also found a red woolen mitten with a leather palm, lying on the ice."

"We had little doubt who had taken it. The only other boat on the river belonged to three hard characters who lived in a shack some twenty miles upstream. We suspected them for some time, as the cattlemen had begun openly threatening to lynch them. They belonged to a class that always holds sway during the raw youth of a frontier community, and the putting down of which is the first step toward decent government."

"Their leader was a well-built fellow named Finnigan, with long red hair reaching to his shoulders, always wearing a broad hat and a fringed buckskin shirt. He had been the chief actor in a number of shooting scrapes. The other two were a half-breed, a stout, muscular man, and an old German, whose viciousness was of the weak and shiftless type."

"We suspected they had taken our boat to escape the area, so we set to work building a flat-bottomed scow to follow them. In any wild country where the power of law is little felt or heeded, men soon get to feel that it is in the highest degree unwise to submit to any wrong. To submit tamely and meekly to theft or to any other injury is to invite almost certain repetition of the offense. No matter the cost of risk or trouble, justice must be done."

"For three days, my two cowboys, Sewall and Dow, and I navigated the icy river, winding through the colorful clay buttes, hoping to take the thieves captive without a fight. A shootout was a concern, for the extraordinary formation of the Badlands, with its cut-up gullies, serried walls, and battlemented hilltops, made it the perfect country for hiding places and ambushes."

"Finally, our watchfulness paid off. On the afternoon of the third day, we came around a bend and spotted our stolen boat moored against the bank. Smoke curled from a campfire among the bushes. We had found the thieves. As I glanced at the faces of my two companions, I saw the grim, eager look in their eyes. Our overcoats were off in a second, and after exchanging a few muttered words, we silently shoved the boat toward the shore."

"As soon as we landed, I ran up behind a clump of bushes to cover the others as they secured the boat. For a moment, excitement thrilled through us as we crept toward the fire, expecting a confrontation. But the only man in camp was the German, and his weapons lay on the ground. He surrendered immediately."

"We secured him and waited for the others. After about an hour, they appeared, walking toward us with rifles slung over their shoulders, the sunlight glinting on the steel barrels. When they were within twenty yards, we straightened from behind the bank, covering them with our cocked rifles. I shouted for them to hold up their hands—an order that, in the West, a man does not disregard if he thinks the giver is in earnest. The half-breed obeyed immediately, his knees trembling, his wolfish eyes darting about. I stepped closer, my rifle aimed at his chest, and repeated the command. With an oath, he let his rifle drop and raised his hands beside his head."

"By this time, they were pretty well cowed, finding quickly that they would be well treated if they behaved but would receive rough handling if they caused trouble. The next morning, we started downriver, heavily laden with our prisoners and the plunder they had gathered. Finnigan, the ringleader, was kept by my side, while the other two were put in their own scow, which was leaky and had only one paddle. We kept them just in front of us, knowing any attempt to escape was hopeless."

"For eight days, we endured the bitter cold, our supplies dwindling. We saw plenty of fresh signs of Sioux activity but managed to avoid them. By the time we reached the C Diamond Ranch, we were low on rations, so we split up. Sewall and Dow continued downriver while I took the prisoners overland to Dickinson."

"I borrowed a pony and hired a settler to drive his wagon with two bronco mares. The settler could hardly understand why I didn't just hang the thieves then and there. Instead, I made them sit in the wagon while I walked behind with my Winchester, ensuring no escape."

"After a grueling thirty-six hours without sleep, we finally jolted into the long, straggling main street of Dickinson. I handed the prisoners over to the sheriff and, under the laws of Dakota, received my fees as a deputy sheriff—amounting to about fifty dollars."

Daniel, who had been hanging on every word, was the first to speak. "Did they hang them?"

Christina's stern voice cut in. "Daniel, that is not appropriate!"

Teddy chuckled. "It's a good question. The answer is no. As a matter of fact, I later received a letter from Mr. Finnigan. He wrote, 'Should you stop over in Bismarck this fall, make a call to the prison. I should be glad to meet you.'"

Daniel glanced at his mother, trying to suppress a grin but knowing better than to say anything else.

Eli, who had been restless throughout the entire conversation, was the first to put on his coat and begin saying his goodbyes.

The ride home was cold, snow falling lightly as they made their way back. Thankfully, Daniel had packed extra blankets in the wagon.

Eli and Christina were quiet, each lost in their thoughts. Meanwhile, Daniel kept the conversation alive, reliving every detail of Teddy's hunting stories, his excitement barely contained.

Chapter 13 – A Journey North

The day after returning from Deadwood, the skies unleashed the full force of winter. Snow fell relentlessly, and temperatures plummeted. Eli and Daniel spent their days battling the elements—hauling firewood, breaking ice in the water troughs, and ensuring the livestock had enough to drink before everything froze solid again.

November bled into December with no relief. Neighbors helped each other dig out from drifts, and the Kind family did their best to keep warm and occupied indoors.

With the harsh weather forcing him inside, Eli found himself dwelling more and more on the information Teddy had shared about Whitey. The pieces were starting to form a picture, and Eli couldn't shake the feeling that he needed to follow up. Using the new telephone—when it actually worked—he tried to track down Teddy. The furthest north he could reach was Belle Fourche, but no one had seen him. Eli figured he was still back East.

His relentless pursuit of answers was beginning to wear on the family. One evening, as he sat at the table, deep in thought, Christina finally spoke.

"I know I'm going to regret saying this," she sighed, "but if the weather breaks, maybe you should just go to Teddy's ranch and find Whitey—put your mind at ease."

A break in the weather came sooner than expected. On December 10th, a Chinook wind roared through, melting the deep snow and nearly causing a flood. With temperatures rising above freezing during the day, Eli knew this was his chance.

Christina, on the other hand, silently hoped he would change his mind. One thing was certain—Daniel was eager to go, but she quickly put an end to that idea. He had already missed too many school days, and besides, she needed him to help with chores.

Eli wasted no time packing supplies. He knew the window of good weather wouldn't last, and the journey was too far to complete in two days. He planned stops in towns along the way in case the weather turned, both for safety and to reassure Christina.

Despite his protests, Daniel was left behind. Christina had given him a heartfelt speech about needing a man around the house, but it was clear from his expression that he was less than impressed with the responsibility.

The weather held, and Eli made good time, though the snow deepened as he traveled north. After three days of steady riding, he finally reached Teddy Roosevelt's Elkhorn Ranch by mid-afternoon.

Elkhorn ranch house

THE KIND REDEMPTION

Teddy had named the ranch after discovering a pair of elk antlers locked together at the site, symbolizing the struggle for survival—a philosophy he held close. The ranch house stood near the river, with a long, low veranda shaded by cottonwoods. From where Eli stood, he could see sandbars and meadows stretching toward a distant line of cliffs and grassy plateaus.

Before he could step onto the veranda, he was met by Wilmot Dow, one of Teddy's trusted ranch hands.

"You must be Eli Kind," Will said, extending a hand.

Eli shook it firmly. "That's right. And you must be Will."

"I've heard a lot about you," Will replied with a grin.

Eli was then introduced to Bill Sewall, another of Teddy's men. While they had never officially met, the names were familiar, and soon the three realized they had crossed paths before—back when Eli was with Sheriff Bullock on the Belle Fourche River.

After some reminiscing, Eli finally got to the reason for his visit. "I was hoping to ask you about Whitey."

Will and Bill exchanged a look before Will said, "Damn, I was hoping you were looking for a job?"

Eli smiled. "No, sorry I am just following up on a lead that Teddy gave me."

Eli waited, hoping for a revelation, but what he got was more of what Teddy had already told him.

"Whitey keeps to himself," Will explained. "Rarely talks to anyone. Works hard, helps with the cattle, and—like Teddy said—he's handy when someone's sick or injured."

Bill nodded in agreement. "He's the best we've got when it comes to doctoring both people and animals. He even helped Teddy after that mess with the boat thieves."

Bill then gestured toward the distant plateau. "See that trail coming out of the bank? That's where Whitey's dug himself a home. He doesn't stay with us at the ranch house—likes his solitude."

Eli studied the ridge. There was a clear path leading from the corral up to a small opening in the hillside.

"He's probably up there now," Will added. "If you want to talk to him, I can ride up and bring him down."

Eli was about to agree when Bill grinned and joked, "Just tell him you've got a woman in need of his services. That'll get him down here quick."

The room chuckled, but Eli could tell this was a bachelor's camp, where crude humor was the norm.

Will excused himself, threw on his coat, and headed toward his horse. As he mounted up, he turned back to Eli. "I'll bring him down. Just sit tight."

Eli nodded, his heart pounding slightly. He had waited a long time for this moment. If Whitey really was Ezra, he was about to find out.

Chapter 14 – Could The Puzzle Find Its Missing Piece?

Eli gazed out the window of the Elkhorn Ranch cabin, watching as Will rode up the trail toward Whitey's dugout bunkhouse. From his vantage point, he could also see how the Little Missouri River split the land the ranch sat on, winding its way through the rugged landscape. Leaning against one of the massive log beams framing the window, he turned to Bill, who was still seated near the fireplace.

"Teddy mentioned that the closest ranch is at least ten miles away?" Eli asked.

Bill nodded. "That's right. And the closest one is still Teddy's—the Maltese Cross Ranch. But the Elkhorn? Will and I built this one ourselves, using cottonwoods from along the river."

Eli glanced around the sturdy, well-built cabin. Though practical and well-constructed, it was clear that no woman had had a hand in its décor.

"Couldn't find any bigger logs?" Eli joked, running his hand along the thick, rough-hewn walls.

Bill chuckled. "Believe it or not, we used the smaller ones. If you look east, downriver, you'll see the real giants we decided not to wrestle into place. These were tough enough."

"You did fine work," Eli said, nodding. "I've built a few homes myself, but nothing using logs this size."

Bill got up, tossing another log onto the fire. "Keeps the weather out and the heat in—especially on days like this."

Eli turned back to the window just in time to catch his first glimpse of Whitey. The old man was following Will up the stone path to the veranda, his white hair stark against the darkening sky. Eli's stomach twisted in knots. He suddenly realized just how unprepared he was for this moment.

Ranch house

What if this man thought he was crazy? What if Whitey truly had no idea what Eli was talking about? And worse... what if he wasn't Ezra at all?

He took a deep breath. Things have a way of working out. Just stay calm. The truth will come.

A moment later, the front door swung open, and Will stepped inside, stamping the muddy snow from his boots.

"This here's Mr. Kind," Will said, pulling off his gloves and unbuttoning his coat. "He's the fella who wanted to see you, Whitey."

Whitey followed, brushing the snow off his coat before reaching out a hand. Eli stepped forward and shook it firmly.

"You can call me Eli," he said. "Nice to meet you."

Whitey nodded. "Likewise, Mr. Kind."

Eli hesitated. "No need to be formal—just Eli is fine."

Whitey shook his head politely. "If you don't object, I'd prefer to address you as Mr. Kind."

Will chuckled. "Don't take offense. He still calls Teddy 'Mr. Roosevelt,' and we all know how much Teddy loves correcting that."

Eli grinned. "No offense taken. And so I properly address you as...?" He paused, waiting for Whitey to fill in the blank.

"Just Whitey, please."

Eli's nerves kicked up again. He had the distinct feeling he was looking into a mirror. Whitey's sharp blue eyes—so much like Eli's own—made this even harder.

This man either truly had no idea who he was... or he was hiding something.

The silence stretched awkwardly. Whitey glanced around the room and shifted uncomfortably before taking a small step toward the door.

"Did I do something wrong?" Whitey asked, his voice cautious.

"No, not at all!" Eli exclaimed. "I'm sorry. I just—" He exhaled sharply. "I need to tell you as much as I know... and see where this goes."

"Please," Eli gestured toward the fireplace, "let's all have a seat, and I'll explain."

Will and Whitey removed their coats and boots, hanging them on the horned coat rack by the door. Once everyone had settled near the fire, Eli wrestled with where to begin.

Maybe some family history?

"My full name is Eli Jacob Kind. My middle name comes from my grandfather, whom I never met, back in Germany. My father, George Kind, came to this country with his two brothers, Charles and Ezra."

Eli watched Whitey closely as he said the name Ezra—but there was no change in Whitey's expression.

Eli swallowed his disappointment and pressed on.

"Charles stayed in Pennsylvania, but my father and Ezra went further west. My father lost track of his brother when they reached Minnesota. That's where he settled, homesteaded, married my mother, and raised me and my sister."

Eli paused, hoping for some sign of recognition.

Whitey shifted uneasily. "So... what does this have to do with me?"

Eli met his gaze. "I was hoping... everything."

A long silence followed. Finally, Will spoke up.

"I get it now. You think Whitey could be your uncle Ezra."

Eli nodded. "Yes... I was hoping that."

Whitey frowned, his expression unreadable. "None of what you said sounds familiar to me."

Disappointment hit Eli like a punch to the gut.

"I—I'm sorry," Eli muttered, standing abruptly. "I knew I should have spoken to Teddy first. I shouldn't have wasted everyone's time."

Whitey, Will, and Bill all protested at once.

Bill stood. "Eli, don't think that way. This must be important for you to come all this way. And don't forget—you're a legend around here yourself. Teddy's always talking about you."

"That's true," Will added with a grin. "Not that Teddy's much of a storyteller."

The room erupted in laughter, and the tension finally eased.

Eli sighed and turned toward the door. "I should go—"

"You're not heading out in this weather," Bill interrupted.

Will crossed his arms. "Not in the dark and not this time of year."

Bill nodded. "Stay the night. We'll make supper after checking on the herd."

Eli hesitated, then nodded. Truth be told, he didn't want to leave. Something still felt unfinished.

Then it hit him.

Reaching into his coat pocket, Eli pulled out the rubbing of the Thoen Stone. Carefully, he unfolded it and held it out.

"Do you recognize this writing?"

Whitey studied it intently.

Will peered over Whitey's shoulder. "Damn. That looks just like your handwriting, Whitey."

Bill frowned. "What is this?"

Eli took a deep breath. "This is a rubbing from the Thoen Stone, found near Spearfish. It has my uncle's name on it... and a very dire message."

Whitey turned the paper in his hands, inspecting it. "This... does look like my writing. But I swear—I don't know anything about it."

Eli pressed on. "I found similar writing on a cave wall in the Ludlow Caves—or what Teddy called the Cave Hills."

The room tensed.

Will turned to Whitey. "That's where I found you, remember? Living in the caves."

Whitey's hands tightened around the paper. He looked around the room uneasily.

"I—I was too embarrassed to admit that," Whitey finally said. "You finding me was the best thing that ever happened to me."

Bill and Will exchanged glances.

Bill spoke first. "Whitey, we've never pried into your past. We all have things we'd rather leave behind. You're one of us now."

Will nodded. "That's right."

Bill glanced at Eli. "I think you two should talk alone."

Whitey exhaled slowly. "I have some chores—"

"No, you don't," Bill interrupted, clapping him on the shoulder. "We got it covered."

As Bill and Will bundled up and headed outside, Eli and Whitey sat in silence, listening to the crackling fire.

Finally, Whitey spoke.

"Mr. Kind... I mean no disrespect, but I don't know where I come from. I don't even think... I have a family."

Eli leaned forward, his heart pounding. "What do you mean?"

Chapter 15 – The Man Behind the Name

"Mr. Kind, I've kept to myself because my life has been confusing—even to me. There are people in my life I feel are family, but I know they're not. I'm about to tell you something I haven't shared with anyone here, not even Mr. Roosevelt. For some reason, I trust you, and I hope I'm not wrong in doing so."

Eli leaned forward. "Whitey, I assure you, I have no intention of harming you or sharing anything you don't want known. I'm only here because I have my own family mystery—one I can't stop trying to solve."

Whitey stood, adding a log to the fire. "I'd better do the only job I was tasked with before I find myself solving the mystery of a new job."

Eli chuckled. "I don't think there's anything you could do to jeopardize your place here. Everyone speaks highly of you."

Whitey sighed. "I hope so, but after what I tell you, I just ask that you be honest with me."

Eli braced himself. He wasn't sure what Whitey was about to reveal, but he had a gut feeling it was something significant.

"I lived with the Lakota and Arikara for many years," Whitey began. "For most of my life, I only knew their language. I did everything with them, and they accepted me as one of their own. But now... now I see how they're treated, and if I tell anyone, I worry I'll be cast out."

Eli's curiosity deepened. "How did you become part of the tribe?"

"That's the part I've thought about a lot." Whitey turned toward the window, his voice quieter. "I believe I was a prisoner at first, but I'm still not sure. I had skills—skills I don't remember learning—but I think they saved my life. And the ones I learned while living with the tribes have kept me alive ever since."

Before Eli could respond, Whitey peered out the window. "But it looks like I'll have to tell you later. Will and Bill are headed this way."

Eli followed his gaze. "I know Teddy well, and he'd never judge you for your past. And I think Will and Bill are reasonable men, too. They might even have their own stories they'd rather not share."

Whitey hesitated, then nodded. "I don't want to lose my place here. I've built a life. But you're right—they deserve to know the truth."

Moments later, Will and Bill stomped through the door, shaking snow off their coats and rushing toward the fireplace.

"Sorry to interrupt, but it's brutal out there!" Will exclaimed.

The burst of cold air sent a chill through the cabin, making both Eli and Whitey instinctively move closer to the fire.

Eli smirked. "Whitey's been on top of the fire all evening, making sure it stays warm enough for you two."

Bill grinned as he pulled off his boots. "Well, as soon as I can feel my fingers again, I say we get something in our bellies. I'll get that beef stew back on the fire—will someone grab the cornbread biscuits from the pantry?"

Whitey raised a hand. "I got it."

As Whitey moved, Eli noticed the way he carried himself—the stiffness in his joints, the signs of a hard-lived life.

Once the table was set and they were all seated, the conversation remained light, mostly about the winter ahead and the cattle. But as Whitey poured fresh coffee for the group, he hesitated, then turned toward them.

"I have something I need to tell you," he said, his voice steady but serious. "Eli traveled all this way looking for answers, and he made me realize I've been avoiding my own. It's time I talk about something I never have before."

Will and Bill exchanged glances, both instantly alert.

Whitey took a breath. "I spent many years living with the Lakota and Arikara, but I have no memory of where I came from... or if I even have a family."

Chapter 16 – Whitey's story

My first memories were of waking up, struggling to open my eyes. My head throbbed so intensely that I almost didn't want to, but I needed to know where I was. I rubbed at my eyelids until the crusted layer of dried blood gave way. Even then, everything remained blurry. I glanced down at my hands—they were covered in dried blood. Panic surged through me as I realized I was lying on my back, staring up at a canopy of wooden poles jutting toward the sky.

As my vision sharpened, I took in my surroundings. The walls around me were made of animal hides, decorated with paintings of creatures I didn't recognize. When I tried to turn my head, a searing pain shot through me, and I let out an involuntary groan. Almost immediately, a gust of wind and a burst of light flooded my vision as someone loomed over me. A man stood there, shouting something I couldn't understand. His voice was harsh, and in his hands, he gripped a heavy wooden club. I flinched, expecting a blow, but as I struggled to move, I realized my hands were free, but my body was tied down.

I fought against the restraints, my groans of pain growing louder. The man raised his club higher, and just when I thought he would strike, a woman rushed in, grabbing his arm. She spoke to him in a scolding tone, and after a moment's hesitation, he wrenched himself free and stormed out of the tent, leaving us alone.

The woman turned her attention to me. Her face was gentle, her touch even more so as she placed a damp cloth against my forehead. The coolness soothed my burning skin, washing away some of the dried blood. She murmured something in a soft, comforting voice, though I couldn't understand her words. Then, she loosened the bindings around my body, propping me up just enough to offer me a small leather pouch. I took it greedily, discovering it held water. I drank deeply, realizing for the first time just how thirsty I was.

Now sitting upright, I could take in more of my surroundings. I was lying on animal furs atop a dirt floor. The structure I was in was circular, supported by long poles tied together at the top, forming a cone. In the center, a small fire smoldered, casting flickering shadows along the hide walls. Near the entrance—just a flap of hide thrown to the side—I could see the bright daylight filtering through.

I tried to speak, but my words were slurred, unrecognizable even to me. My head ached so terribly that I could barely think. I let my eyes close again, surrendering to the darkness.

When I awoke next, the room was dimly lit, the fire casting a warm glow. Across from me, the woman sat watching, her face illuminated in the soft flicker of the flames. She had cared for me through my fevered days, patiently nursing me back to health. Over time, I learned her name—Ska'u—and noticed that she was pregnant. Though we could not communicate at first, we managed with gestures.

She called me "Titaree," and for a long time, I assumed that was my name. But beyond that, I knew nothing. I had no memory of how I'd come to be here or what had happened to me. I only knew that my body was bruised and broken—my ribs aching more than my head— and that I was some kind of prisoner. Ska'u was the only reason I was still alive.

The village was small, about twenty teepees in total. Whenever Ska'u helped me outside, I could feel the weight of a hundred eyes on me. The only person who spoke directly to me was a man named

Kȟaŋǧí Yátapi—Ska'u's husband. Unlike her, he was cold and distant, often muttering things I did not understand but could tell were not in my favor. He had wanted to leave me for dead, and perhaps he still wished that had been the case.

As I healed, Ska'u taught me more of their language. She told me that Kȟaŋǧí and his warriors had found me half-dead on a high hill, left to die by the Arikara, who had been camped below near the creek. The name meant nothing to me, nor did the details of my supposed attack. My past was an empty void, and I had no choice but to piece things together from what little I was given.

Then, one night, Ska'u went into labor. I woke to her pained moans from across the fire. Instinct took over—I knew exactly what to do. I helped deliver her son just as the sun rose over the horizon.

That morning, when Ska'u stepped out of the teepee cradling her newborn, the village's perception of me changed. I was no longer just a burden—I had saved her child. Even Kȟaŋǧí treated me with a shred more tolerance, though I knew he still resented me. They named the child Tȟamila Wewe, and as the days passed, I found myself settling into life with the Lakota.

But there was always a part of me that felt separate, an outsider looking in.

Years passed as the village moved with the seasons, following the herds. Then, one day, while camped along the banks of the Red River, I heard something that sent a jolt through me—voices speaking a language I understood.

Two men in rawhide clothes were trading buffalo hides for guns with Kȟaŋǧí. When they turned to speak to one another, I recognized the words. English.

I froze. The realization that I could understand them, that their language was familiar to me, was overwhelming. I wanted to run to them, to ask them where I belonged, but I knew that if I interrupted Kȟaŋǧí, I might be thrown into the trade myself. Instead, I went to Ska'u and told her what I had heard.

She told me the men were from a fort many miles away, near the Big Muddy River. The idea of following them, of finding out who I was, burned inside me, but I held back. I owed Ska'u my life, and I couldn't abandon her.

But fate had other plans.

More time passed, and eventually, tensions in the village grew. Ska'u's son, Tȟamila, had grown into a young warrior but was treated with disdain by others in the tribe, particularly by a boy named Gall. The mistreatment worried Ska'u, and she confided in me her fears for Tȟamila's future. She wanted to leave—to take her son back to her Arikara people.

I knew it was dangerous. If we were caught, it would mean certain death. But I owed Ska'u everything.

One night, under the full moon, we slipped away.

By late the next day, we were within sight of the camp when two braves on horseback intercepted us. Their initial reaction was to kill me on the spot, but after recognizing Ska'u, they allowed her to speak. She explained our struggles, and after some tense moments, we were welcomed into the village.

As we settled in, I couldn't help but wonder—had anyone in this tribe played a role in my injuries? When I finally voiced my concerns to Ska'u, she reassured me. She explained that while her people had a faction of warriors who sought to drive out all intruders, that group had since split off and established themselves elsewhere. There was no need to worry.

I quickly fell into a familiar rhythm, tending to the sick and injured while also working in the expansive gardens near the creek. Thamila adapted just as well, making friends with ease. Ska'u often commented on how happy he seemed, relieved that he no longer had to endure the torment of Gall's bullying.

During this time, Ska'u taught me the Arikara language. Since I had already learned Lakota, communication became much easier. I was also introduced to Skataaka, a man who spoke the language of the traders from the fort. The first time I heard him speak, something inside me clicked. Words I hadn't known I remembered came rushing back. Before long, I was conversing with Skataaka as if I had known English all my life.

He explained that it was the language of the white man, taught to him when his tribe had lived near the fort on the Big Muddy. He had been taken in by the Arikara after marrying into the tribe and now served as their primary trader with the fort.

Seasons passed, and I dedicated myself to learning all I could about the white men from Skataaka. At the same time, I taught Thamila what I had learned, knowing it would serve him well.

Life in the village was good. Ska'u had remarried and had two more sons, both of whom were growing into strong young warriors like their older brother. The crops flourished, better than I had ever seen, and I found myself helping to negotiate trades with the men from the fort.

Still, the pull to visit the fort myself lingered in the back of my mind. Yet when I brought it up, one of the traders warned me that I would not be welcome after having lived among the Arikara. At the time, I didn't understand why.

Then, everything changed.

Thamila and I had just finished harvesting vegetables near the creek when the distant crack of gunfire shattered the quiet afternoon.

Screams followed.

THE KIND REDEMPTION

We dropped our baskets and ran toward the village, arriving just in time to see bodies strewn across the ground. Teepees were ablaze, their flames licking the sky.

Our first instinct was to find Ska'u. We sprinted to her teepee, only to find her kneeling over the lifeless bodies of her two youngest sons.

Thamila rushed to her side, gripping her tightly. Between sobs, she pointed toward the horizon, her voice shrill with grief.

"Gall! Gall!"

The name sent a cold wave of rage through me. Gall had led this attack, killing Ska'u's children along with ten others. They had stolen as much of the harvest as they could carry, setting fire to the storage teepees holding the rest.

The village was in ruins.

It took every ounce of my strength to restrain Thamila from charging after them. He swore vengeance, his fury barely contained. But it was suicide. The Lakota were stronger than ever, and any attempt to strike back would only end in more bloodshed.

With no food, no security, and no way to fight back, the decision was made. Those who survived would pack up what little remained and travel to join another Arikara tribe a day's journey away.

But for Thamila, it wasn't enough. His anger was beyond Ska'u's control, and I knew if I didn't intervene, he would be lost to revenge.

And so, it was decided.

Thamila and I would leave together.

We would forge our own path.

We ventured north, traveling cautiously and only under the cover of night, knowing we were heading in the direction of the Lakota village. By the next day, we reached a place of shelter just north of the Slim Buttes. We called it *kaniťš*, named after the sharpening stone used by the women of the tribes for their awls, a feature of the main cave.

All the tribes knew of *kaniťš*, but only the *winyan*, the women, ever came there. They never spoke of our presence, and in time, they even brought us small gifts. The hunting was plentiful year-round, and we established multiple places to call home, never staying in one spot too long. We never knew who might stumble upon us, so we had to be prepared.

There were close calls. Occasionally, braves would come too near, but we learned to use the cave's natural echoes and eerie sounds to scare them away. They believed the caves to be part of the underworld, and that belief kept us safe.

For over a year, we remained there, living in the shadows of the land, until one day, Thamila proposed something that changed everything.

He wanted to go to the fort on the Big Muddy.

I resisted at first. Something about it unsettled me in a way I couldn't explain. But Thamila was obsessed. If I refused, I knew he would go alone—or worse, hunt down Gall himself. So, I agreed.

The journey to the fort was long, and the closer we got, the more uneasy I became.

Then, the moment I stepped inside its boundaries, something inside me stirred. My memories, long buried, began to surface in flashes—objects, places, words. I knew what I was looking at, yet I couldn't remember why or how. It frightened me. People watched us with suspicion, and I felt an overwhelming urge to leave.

While I wrestled with my own ghosts, Thamila found purpose.

A soldier—newly returned from what he called the *Civil War*—was looking for an Indian to carry mail for the government. He had no idea that Thamila spoke English, and when my friend answered him fluently, the soldier was visibly shocked.

He explained the job, and to my surprise, Thamila agreed to sign up that very day.

I never thought he'd go through with it. But as the sun set, I found myself leaving the fort alone, riding back to *kanitš* without him.

Life returned to a quiet routine.

I spent my days in solitude, marking the walls of the cave with my winter counts, passing time as best I could. Twice, the seasons changed before I saw Thamila again.

He was the only one who could approach *kanitš* without me noticing. His sudden arrival was a welcome surprise.

Still carrying mail for the government, he told me he had been reassigned from Fort Clark to Fort Abraham Lincoln. It was closer, meaning he could visit more often. I was glad for it—*winyan* no longer came to *kanitš*, and I had grown too accustomed to the quiet.

Thamila laughed, saying it was because the story of *the crazy man with the white bushy beard* had spread across all the tribes.

Eli had been listening intently, but now, he could no longer hold back.

"Fort Abraham Lincoln?" he interrupted.

"Yes," Whitey continued. "He didn't return again until late that fall, just before winter. That's when he told me he was going to be a scout for an expedition in the spring."

Eli sat forward. "Spring of '74?"

Whitey thought for a moment, then nodded. "Yes, I believe so. Soldiers passed through *kanit* and wrote their names on the cave walls. Some of them marked the year—'74.' I saw them coming before they got close, heard their music playing. I hid in one of the deeper caves until they left. Later, Thamila told me he stayed at the camp and warned them about *the crazy man living in the caves.*"

Eli shot up from his seat, eyes wide.

"I was there! We were there!" Eli points to Whitey and continues. That is your writing on the walls. I was that close to you in '74 and didn't even know it! I didn't go to the caves because my friend Bloody Knife told me they were haunted by a madman! When the soldiers came back, they said they didn't see anyone, so I never thought about it again."

Whitey tugged at his white beard and studied Eli carefully.

"Did you say your friend *Bloody Knife?*"

"Yes." Eli's voice was quieter now. "Bloody Knife was a scout for the 7th Cavalry under General Custer. He was my friend."

Whitey's expression softened as he turned toward Will and Bill, then back to Eli.

"Bloody Knife," he said, his voice heavy with emotion, "was Thamila."

Eli slowly sank back into his seat, hands covering his face as the weight of the revelation settled over him.

"How can this be?" he murmured.

Whitey continued; his voice quiet but steady.

"I told you—he was given the Lakota name *Thamila Wewe*. It means *Bloody Knife*. He was like a son to me."

Eli swallowed hard. "And he was my best friend."

A long silence hung between them before Whitey finally asked, "You know what happened to him, then?"

Eli hesitated, then looked up, meeting Whitey's eyes.

"I do. He was killed at Little Bighorn. I would have been there too—if I had re-enlisted that year."

Whitey blinked hard, his aging blue eyes glistening as he held back tears.

"I saw what happened," he whispered.

Eli's breath caught in his throat.

"You were *there?*"

Whitey nodded; his voice heavy with sorrow.

"I was there."

It wasn't long after your expedition passed me again that Thamila—Bloody Knife—came to warn me. The tribes were converging, and the army was growing nervous. He had been in touch with his mother, Ska'u, and told me that they were moving toward a place called *Greasy Grass*. The army was planning to round up the tribes and force them onto reservations, but he knew there would be a fight.

I wanted to see Ska'u again, to try and talk them out of it, but when I arrived at *Greasy Grass*, I quickly realized there was no stopping what was coming. Crazy Horse, Sitting Bull, and Gall had had enough of running. They were ready for war.

I had never seen anything like it before—a vast village of tribes united in purpose, working together despite their differences. It was an incredible sight, but it carried an ominous weight. I knew I could do nothing to change their minds.

After speaking with Ska'u, I decided to leave before the fighting began. As I reached the stream at the village's edge, the first shots rang out.

I ducked behind a massive cottonwood tree and saw warriors pouring out of the village, charging toward the gunfire. The soldiers had advanced from the east, moving through the trees at the bottom of the coulee. Smoke filled the air, and through the chaos, I heard a familiar voice.

Thamila!

THE KIND REDEMPTION

Through the haze, I saw him—standing among the soldiers, trying to direct them, trying to keep them from being overrun. He shouted for them to retreat, but before he could turn to the officer beside him, a bullet struck him in the back of the head. Blood sprayed across the officer, who barely had time to react before the retreat began.

The soldiers fled. The warriors pursued.

I ran to Thamila, desperate to reach him, but I was too late.

I turned back toward the village, hoping to find Ska'u, but before I could reach her, I ran into a French trapper. He was waving his rifle wildly, calling for me to help him fire at the soldiers. I shoved past him, saying I had to find my friend, and he disappeared up the coulee.

It was chaos. Warriors and soldiers clashed, gunshots echoed, smoke and dust filled the air.

Not long after, the warriors returned, victorious, riding the soldiers' stolen horses and wearing their jackets in triumph. I finally found Ska'u and told her about Thamila.

She demanded to see his body.

By the time we got there, it was too late. The warriors had beheaded him, his severed head mounted on a pole as a warning to traitors.

Ska'u broke down, sobbing louder than the victory chants that filled the village.

I took her back to her *teepee*. That was the last time I ever saw her.

I knew I had to leave. More soldiers would come, and I wanted no part in what would happen next. That night, under cover of darkness, I slipped away and traveled alone.

Eli, Will and Bill sat in stunned silence as Whitey continued.

I reached *kaniť* late the next afternoon. But it wasn't the same.

The memories of Thamila, of Ska'u, of all I had lost haunted me. I couldn't stay there anymore.

I knew Thamila had wed an Arikara woman named Young Owl Woman. He fathered a daughter and two sons. The daughter died of an illness and was buried at Fort Buford. One son was killed in a raid by Lakota on the Arikara village. I wanted to find the only son he had left but did not know where to look.

I had no plan, no direction—until I saw a stray cow wandering along the bluff while I was out hunting.

Herds of cattle had passed through before, but they never stopped. I had paid them little mind. But this one? It seemed like an easy hunt.

Then, in the distance, I saw a rider approaching.

I tensed, wary of his intentions. I had already started forming a story in my mind—if he accused me of stealing the cow, I would insist I was looking for its rightful owner.

As the man drew closer, he raised his hands in a gesture of peace. I did the same.

Bill suddenly interrupted. "Wait, I know this part! This is when I found you wandering around the Cave Hills, right?"

Will shot Bill a playful punch on the arm. "Let him tell it, will ya? Don't ruin the story!"

Whitey ignored them, his focus on the memory.

He thanked me for finding the cow, and I pretended that had been my intention all along. He explained that his group was moving cattle to Belle Fourche, and this was the last stray they needed to recover after a storm scattered part of the herd the night before.

Then he asked, "Are you from around here?"

I hesitated.

For some reason, I told him I was heading to Belle Fourche to find work.

I hadn't planned to say it. The words just came out.

He smiled and said, "If you know anything about cattle, we could use an extra hand."

Then he reached out his hand.

"My name's Will." Whitey then looks at Will and nods at him as Will proudly puffs out his chest and smiles.

I hesitated again. I didn't know what name to give him. If I said *Titaree*, he would suspect me of being an Indian.

So, I mumbled something that must have sounded like *Whitey*.

He repeated it with a nod, and just like that, *Whitey* became my name.

Before I could think twice, I was on his horse, helping drive the stray cow back to camp.

That's when I met the herd's owner.

Mr. Roosevelt.

He welcomed me to the fire, handed me a plate of food, and introduced me to the rest of the cowboys. Each one stepped forward to shake my hand.

I had never known such kindness.

I had found my place.

Soon, I settled in as the herd's medicine man, caring for the cattle and the cowboys alike.

I rode on several drives, and some of the men took to calling me *Doc*—though *Whitey* was the name that stuck.

Mr. Roosevelt has been good to me. He gave me a home, a purpose.

A second chance.

A chance at a good life at the Elkhorn Ranch.

> I am old now and I have my routine that keeps me busy and
> happy on the ranch as long as he will have me

Chapter 17 - Echoes of the Past, Questions of the Present

When Whitey finished speaking, he looked around the table, searching for a reaction. But all that filled the silence was the crackling fire and the wind howling outside.

Finally, Eli broke the quiet. "Whitey, I don't have any ill feelings toward you or the way you've lived your life. Your choices were about survival, and I understand that."

Will and Bill nodded in agreement, and Will added, "I always figured you had an interesting backstory, but I had no idea it ran this deep."

Whitey let out a slow breath. "I've never told all of it to anyone before—it just came out the best I could remember."

"But you really don't remember where you came from? Or who your family is?" Will asked, his brow furrowed.

"Were you sleeping when he said that in the beginning?" Bill shot back, shaking his head.

Will scowled at him. "No, I heard it. I just don't understand how someone could forget something like that."

Bill questioned. "Ever heard of amnesia? He literally said he was hit on the head. Were you still sleeping then?"

Eli took the opportunity to jump in. "That actually could explain a lot. Maybe you did carve your name into the stone, and the amnesia is why you don't remember it."

Whitey's expression tensed. "Eli, as much as I'd like to help you with your family mystery, I don't have any memory of that stone."

Bill suddenly perked up. "I've heard people with amnesia can sometimes regain their memories if they visit familiar places. Something about triggering lost connections."

Will smirked and seized the moment. "Oh, like how every time we go to town, you conveniently forget your money, so I have to pay? That amnesia never seems to wear off."

They all laughed, and Bill chuckled. "I just don't remember that happening."

The laughter died down, and Eli turned back to Whitey. "Seriously, though—I've heard the same thing. Would you consider traveling back to where the stone was found?"

Whitey hesitated, glancing at Will and Bill before responding. "My place is here. I don't want to risk losing that."

Both Will and Bill started talking at once, overlapping in their eagerness to reassure him. Finally, Will took the lead. "Look, we don't have a problem with you taking the trip. But, uh… where exactly are we talking about?"

Eli nodded. "It was found near Spearfish, on a hillside called Lookout Mountain. Not far from my ranch." He paused before adding, "My ranch was a stage stop before the railroad made the line to Deadwood. If you're willing, I know my wife Christina, my son Daniel, and I would be honored to have you stay with us. Actually, we'd love to have you for Christmas—it's coming up fast."

Eli could see Whitey tense at the idea of leaving, so he softened his approach. "I know this is a lot to consider. You don't have to decide right now—just think about it."

Bill jumped in, grinning. "Actually, this might be the perfect time for you to go. Things are slow at the ranch, and you know how boring Christmas is around here anyway."

Will folded his arms and scoffed. "What do you mean? We already have our Christmas tree." He nodded toward the half-dead stick in the corner.

Eli had noticed it when he arrived, assuming it was meant for kindling, but now he felt a twinge of guilt realizing it held some meaning.

"And here I thought my caroling was the highlight of the season," Will added with a grin.

Whitey smirked. "Now that you mention it, I do have some memories of Christmas songs—somehow, I know the words, but I don't remember learning them."

Will grinned. "Must be my great singing."

Whitey shook his head but let the moment settle before continuing. "I don't know what triggers certain memories—sometimes it's music, sometimes reading books Mr. Roosevelt gave me. Maybe going back would help unlock more." He looked at Will and Bill. "If you two are really fine with it, I wouldn't mind taking Eli up on his offer."

Will and Bill exchanged glances before nodding in unison. "Go for it," Will said.

Eli felt a mix of excitement and uncertainty. How would he explain this to Christina? What if Whitey wasn't Ezra? And what if he was? He shook off the questions for now—this was an experiment, and he'd deal with the consequences later.

Looking at Whitey, he asked, "Would you be ready to leave at first light tomorrow, or do you need more time?"

Whitey glanced at Will and Bill, who were both nodding encouragingly. "I'll be ready."

"Good," Eli said, standing. "I don't trust the weather this time of year, so I want to get going while it's still decent."

Whitey excused himself to pack, leaving the others to finish cleaning up.

After the meal was cleared away, Bill showed Eli to his bunk in the back of the cabin. The fire crackled softly, the wind still howling outside. Within minutes, the cabin was quiet, save for the occasional creak of settling logs.

Tomorrow, they'd set off on a journey into the unknown.

Would it bring answers—or more questions?

Chapter 18 – The Ride Back to Answers?

E li was up before dawn, and so was the rest of the cabin. He noticed the glow of a lantern in the dugout where Whitey lived, a small light in the predawn darkness. As he pulled on his coat, he turned to Will and Bill.

"I hope this isn't going to be a problem. I didn't come here to take help away from you."

Will was the first to respond. "If this trip brings any amount of peace to either one of you, it'll be worth it for all of us."

Bill nodded in agreement, and Eli sighed, rubbing his hands together for warmth. "I don't even know how to handle this, except to see if Whitey remembers anything along the way."

"That's all you can do," Bill said.

As Eli and Will bundled up, Bill handed him a sack. "I packed some food to get you down the trail, but we should get you a few more hide-covered canteens. Water's only getting harder to find."

Eli took the sack with a nod of gratitude. "Yeah, I had to break through ice on the way here, and it's only getting thicker."

By the time they reached the barn, Whitey had joined them. There was little talk as they saddled up, the crisp morning air biting at their faces. The horses stomped and snorted, eager to get moving. With final goodbyes and words of caution, they set off just as the first rays of sun stretched across the horizon.

Looking back at the Elkhorn Ranch, Eli took in the rolling hills, cottonwood groves along the river, and the deep-cut ravines. It was a spectacular sight, and he understood why Teddy Roosevelt had fallen in love with the land.

"It sure is a pretty morning," Eli commented.

Whitey, his breath curling in the air, glanced back at the ranch. "Yeah, but I wouldn't mind it being a little warmer."

The two rode at an easy pace, navigating the rough, uneven terrain—hard-packed clay, loose rock, and sandy soil, with patches of grass peeking through the snow. Junipers and cottonwoods stood in the more sheltered areas, their branches bending under the weight of frost.

Eli frequently asked if they were on the best route, and Whitey always gave the same answer. "This land is pretty much the same no matter which way you go."

By midday, the landscape transitioned into rolling prairie, vast and open. The wind picked up, biting at their exposed skin, and Eli was grateful when Whitey suggested a more sheltered path through a natural drainage. The difference was immediate—the wind still swirled in the ravine, but it was bearable.

"Good call," Eli said, flexing his fingers inside his gloves. "I can feel my hands again."

Whitey nodded, his beard already coated in ice, making it impossible to read his expression.

They found patches of ice-thin enough to break for the horses to drink, and by late afternoon, plateaus rose on the horizon. Whitey pointed southeast. "That canyon leads straight to the stage line. From there, we'll hit Ludlow."

"Perfect," Eli said. "I was hoping we'd get there before dark."

They reached the Ludlow stage stop just as the sun dipped below the horizon. After stabling the horses, they checked into the stagehouse, where the warmth of the fire and the smell of stew were a welcome relief. Whitey excused himself to knock the ice from his beard outside, while Eli silently critiqued the accommodations—it wasn't much, but it was warm.

After a hot meal and much-needed rest, they were back on the trail before dawn, following the well-worn stage line south. The morning was cold, and by the time the sun had fully risen, Whitey's beard was once again frozen.

As they rode, Whitey pointed to a butte in the distance. "There's a story about that place. The Arikara wiped out an entire tribe of Crow Indians here. The old warriors used to talk about it, said the bodies are still out there."

The story made Eli pick up the pace. He didn't like the feeling of being so exposed out on the plains—he knew they were likely being watched.

The day was easier than the last, and Eli briefly considered shedding a layer, but as the sun sank lower, so did the temperature. Their goal was to reach Redig before nightfall, and they made it with time to spare. Though tempted to keep going, Eli knew the next shelter was too far. The promise of a hot meal and a warm bed at the Redig hotel was too good to pass up.

They were back on the trail well before sunrise. Eli was determined to make it home that night. The land remained unchanged—wide, rolling prairie with the occasional butte breaking the horizon. The snow was getting deeper, but luck was on their side—they found a creek where someone had already broken the ice, saving them precious time.

Eli kept the conversation light, discussing the trail, the weather, and possible encounters with tribes. Though he wanted to tell Whitey more about Ezra, he decided to wait until they reached the ranch—maybe Christina could help with the approach.

Just as the Black Hills came into view, an ominous gray cloud spread across the western sky. Without a word, both men urged their horses into a faster pace.

By the time they reached Belle Fourche, the snow was falling in thick, heavy flakes. Visibility dropped to near nothing.

Eli led them to the stockyards, where he had made calls before. Inside, Tom Wellington was behind the counter, looking up in surprise as they stomped in, shaking off the snow.

"Eli Kind! I suppose you're here to tell the missus you'll be sleeping in a snowdrift tonight?" Tom grinned.

Eli brushed more snow from his coat. "Not if I can help it. Just wanted to let her know I'm on the way."

Tom cast a glance out the window. "Well, make it quick. This storm's not letting up."

As Eli made his way to the telephone, Tom turned his attention to Whitey.

"I've seen you around, but I don't believe I caught your name. You're with the Elkhorn bunch, right?"

Eli froze. He hadn't planned this introduction. Before Whitey could answer, Eli stepped in. "Tom, this is my friend Whitey. He works up at Elkhorn. I invited him to spend Christmas with us."

Tom extended a hand. "Nice to meet you again, Whitey."

Whitey shook his hand. "Likewise."

Eli got through to Christina, who was overjoyed to hear his voice. "You're coming home in this storm?"

"We'll be fine," Eli assured her. "And I'm bringing a friend."

"Is it Ezra?"

Eli hesitated. He lowered his voice, glancing at Whitey. "It's... a long story. Trust me, you'll understand when I get there."

"That's his name? Whitey?"

Eli sighed. "Like I said, long story. We'll see you soon."

Christina relented, though he could hear the curiosity in her voice. "Be careful. I love you."

"I love you too."

Eli hung up and turned to Tom. "Thanks, Tom. I'll let you know when we make it."

Tom nodded. "You two be careful out there."

Back outside, the wind howled, snow whipping into their faces. As they mounted up, Eli rode up beside Whitey.

"Back there with Tom—I hope that was okay. I didn't know what else to say."

Whitey gave a slight nod, his frozen beard making it impossible to see his expression. "It's fine. I'm your friend from Elkhorn, spending Christmas with you."

Eli smiled. "Sounds good to me."

With that, they turned toward Spearfish, pushing through the worsening storm, determined to reach home before nightfall.

Like Eli had said, the road was easy to follow, though the snow was getting deeper. Along the way, they passed a few wagons and met travelers heading back toward Belle Fourche, their quick pace suggesting they were trying to outrun the worsening storm.

Eli explained to Whitey that, on a clear day, the mountains of the Black Hills would dominate the horizon. But with the heavy snowfall, they could barely see ten feet ahead. The wind picked up, making things even worse. Eli felt the chill seep through his layers, and he wondered how Whitey was faring. Then again, Whitey had already proven he could handle the cold better than Eli.

It came as a surprise when the outline of buildings emerged through the swirling white. Eli reoriented himself and rode closer to Whitey. "Stay close. We'll warm up at the hardware store just down the street."

They made their way through town, the buildings offering some shelter from the wind. At Cashner Hardware, Eli swung down and held the door open as they rushed inside, stomping snow from their boots.

John Cashner looked up from behind the counter, eyebrows raised. "What are you doing out in this weather, Eli?"

Eli shook the snow from his coat. "Coming back from the Elkhorn Ranch in North Dakota—didn't expect the weather to hit this hard." He turned toward Whitey, motioning toward him. "John, this is my friend Whitey. He's one of the cowboys up at Elkhorn. I invited him to spend Christmas with us."

John extended his hand. "Pleasure to meet you, Whitey. Isn't Elkhorn Teddy's place?"

Whitey nodded as they shook hands. "Yes, Mr. Roosevelt's operation."

John shot Eli a knowing look. "And you dragged him all the way here in this weather? I know the bunkhouse Christmas might not be the first choice, but it's probably warmer."

Eli glanced at Whitey, but his expression was unreadable beneath the ice-coated beard. Wanting to keep the conversation moving, Eli changed the subject. "You got any of that jerky left from this fall?"

"I do," John replied. "How much you need?"

"Cut off a few slabs for us now and wrap up two pounds to take home."

"Sure thing," John said, disappearing into the back room.

Eli turned to Whitey, who was wandering the store, taking in the variety of goods. "John keeps just about everything in here. He's even got a meat locker in the back. George Stabler, our local butcher, shares it with him, so there's always fresh meat."

Whitey nodded, still looking around, as John returned, carrying the jerky. "Here you go," he said, handing Eli the fresh slabs and the

111

wrapped package. "Not to rush you out, but this storm doesn't look like it's letting up anytime soon."

Eli paid for the jerky and then asked, "Did you move Louis's stone?"

John shook his head. "No. He came and picked it up the other day. Said he wanted to study it more. Why do you ask?"

"I was hoping to show Whitey, but we'd better get going."

Whitey had drifted toward the back of the store, but at Eli's call, he walked up and took the jerky Eli handed him. They said their goodbyes and stepped back into the storm, mounting their snow-covered horses.

"The ranch isn't far," Eli told Whitey. "We'll follow the buildings through town while we can."

The shelter of town helped block the wind, but as soon as they reached the outskirts, the full force of the storm hit them. The wind howled, the snow stung like needles, and visibility was nearly nonexistent.

They followed the railroad tracks east, the path barely visible beneath the drifts. As the snow deepened, they dismounted and led their horses, feeling their way along the tracks. Several times, they veered too close to the edge, nearly losing their footing.

Eli's sense of direction wavered. Had they gone too far? Was there anything familiar to help him find his bearings? His mind played tricks on him, and for a moment, panic threatened to creep in.

He kept glancing at Whitey. "You holding up?"

Whitey only grunted in response, his face lost behind a mask of snow and ice.

Eli wondered what Whitey was thinking—whether he regretted coming, whether he resented Eli for leading him into this mess. He had survived all these years, only to risk dying in a blizzard with a man chasing ghosts.

Just then, Eli's foot struck something solid. He reached out, running his gloved hands over the surface. A milepost. Relief flooded him.

"We made it!" he shouted. "This is my ranch. The fence should be about twenty feet ahead."

With renewed energy, they pushed forward through the snow. Just as Eli predicted, the top wire of the fence emerged from the drifts. Eli stepped on it, pressing it down as Whitey led the horses over.

Mounting up again, they plowed through the final stretch until a familiar shape materialized in the distance.

"That's my barn!" Eli hollered over the wind.

The doors, thankfully, were free of snow. They led the horses inside, the warmth and shelter a welcome relief. After making sure the animals were settled, Eli turned toward the house, barely visible through the storm.

"Come on," he said, motioning to Whitey. "Let's get inside."

Chapter 19 - Through the Blizzard to Family and Fate

The chill that had settled deep in Eli's bones vanished the moment he stepped through the front door. Christina was already rushing toward him, still wearing her flour-dusted cooking apron. He barely had time to shrug off his half-frozen coat before she threw her arms around his neck, holding him tight.

"I know I should trust your judgment," she murmured, relief in her voice, "but I was really starting to worry."

As she finally pulled back, her eyes landed on the tall, snow-covered figure standing behind Eli.

"Oh! Where are my manners?" She quickly straightened herself and extended a hand. "You must be Whitey."

Whitey shifted uncomfortably but took her hand with a nod. "Yes, ma'am."

Christina clasped his hand with both of hers. "You're still frozen." She turned back to Eli. "You both must be. I just sent Daniel into the dining room to stoke up the fire. Give me your coats, go warm yourselves up."

Eli and Whitey peeled off their heavy, ice-laden garments, handing them to Christina. As they turned toward the dining room, Eli barely had time to react before a blur of movement crashed into him.

"Dad! You're finally home!" Daniel shouted, gripping his father in a fierce hug.

Eli grinned, ruffling his son's hair. "Yes, I am! And we'll catch up soon, but first, I'd like to introduce you to someone."

Daniel let go and straightened as Eli gestured toward Whitey. "Daniel, this is Whitey. Whitey, meet my son, Daniel."

Daniel extended his hand, but his eyes flickered with uncertainty as he stammered, "It's... it's nice to meet you, Mr. Wh-Wh-Whitey."

Whitey looked down at him and, for the first time, Eli thought he saw the hint of a smile behind the ice-crusted beard. "Nice to meet you, Mr. Daniel."

Daniel beamed, shaking Whitey's hand with more confidence before Christina called him to help in the kitchen.

A few minutes later, mother and son returned—Daniel balancing a plate of cookies while Christina carried a steaming coffee pot. They set everything down on the table, and Christina announced, "Once you two thaw out, I figured you could use something warm, with a little treat to go with it."

Eli wrapped his hands around the cup she handed him, savoring the warmth. "Thank you. It sure is good to be home."

Whitey gave a small nod of thanks, but remained quiet, absorbing the room.

Just then, Eli remembered his promise to call Tom once he made it home. He shot up from his chair and headed straight for the phone, calling over his shoulder, "I'll be right back." Christina, sensing urgency, followed him, wondering if something was wrong.

Eli cranked the handle on the phone, and after a brief pause, a voice came through the receiver. "Who would you like to speak with?"

"Tom Wellington, please," Eli responded.

As he waited, he turned to Christina, covering the mouthpiece with his hand. "I told Tom I'd call when we got in. I don't want him sending someone out to look for us."

Christina gave him an approving nod just as Tom's familiar voice came through the line. "I hope this is Eli calling because I sure wasn't expecting anyone else."

Eli let out a small chuckle. "It's me, Tom. We made it. It's late, so I won't keep you—I just wanted to say thank you and wish you a Merry Christmas."

"Well, that's good to hear," Tom replied warmly. "Merry Christmas to you, too."

With that, Eli hung up the phone and returned to the dining room, sliding back into his seat, relieved to have kept his word.

As they sat together at the dining table, Eli spoke first. "I have to thank you both for the welcome home. And for clearing the barn door so we could get the horses in right away."

Christina reached over and squeezed Daniel's hand proudly. "That was all this young man's doing. He told me he was going to shovel a path to the barn to make sure his dad could get inside when he arrived. He even brought in all the wood and kept the fire going strong."

Eli's chest swelled with pride. "Thank you, son. That was a big help—we had enough of that weather."

Daniel blushed but tried to play it off. "Well, Mom was busy baking treats, so I needed something to do."

Christina chuckled, giving his shoulder a squeeze.

After another sip of coffee, Eli turned toward Whitey. "Now that we're all a bit more comfortable, I want to officially welcome Whitey to our home. He works for Uncle Teddy up at the Elkhorn Ranch, and after some convincing, he agreed to come spend Christmas with us."

Christina's smile widened. "That's wonderful. Welcome, Whitey— we're happy to have you."

Whitey shifted in his chair, clearly unaccustomed to such warmth. He cleared his throat and said softly, "Thank you for having me. You have a beautiful home. I feel... lucky to be here."

The conversation drifted to stories of the Elkhorn Ranch, the journey through the blizzard, and life on the plains. Eli did most of the talking while Whitey seemed content to listen, offering only a nod when Daniel asked if he could visit the ranch someday.

Noticing Whitey's quiet demeanor, Eli decided it was time to call it a night. "I think we could all use some rest. Hopefully, the storm lets up so you can see more of the ranch tomorrow."

Eli and Daniel led Whitey upstairs to one of the old stagecoach guest rooms. Daniel excitedly pointed out the multiple beds and the small washbasin. "This used to be for stagecoach travelers," he explained. "You even get your own sink! My room's right across the hall, so if you need anything, I can show you around in the morning."

Whitey gave a small nod of appreciation.

Eli clapped Daniel on the back. "Goodnight, son."

Daniel grinned. "Goodnight, Dad! Goodnight, Mr. Whitey!"

117

Whitey simply nodded again before stepping inside his room, closing the door behind him.

Eli made his way back to the kitchen, where Christina was finishing up the last of the dishes. He leaned against the counter and asked, "Need any help?"

She shook her head. "No, I'm nearly done. You need to get some rest. Go get ready for bed—I'll be up in a minute."

Eli kissed her forehead before heading off. As he walked away, she called after him, "A man of few words, that Whitey."

Eli smiled. "You have no idea—yet."

By the time they climbed into bed, Christina was full of questions, just as Eli had expected. He told her everything he knew about Whitey—the mystery of his past, his time with the tribes, the possibility that he might be someone they had been searching for all along.

Christina listened carefully, her brow furrowed in thought. "Bringing him here might help him remember," she admitted. "But Eli, don't get your hopes up too high. You don't want to be disappointed."

He sighed. "I know. I keep telling myself that, but something in my gut tells me I needed to bring him here."

Christina exhaled and snuggled closer, wrapping an arm around him. "I trust your gut. Just take it one day at a time."

She fell quiet for a moment before adding playfully, "You do realize you just brought a total stranger into my house—across the hall from my son?"

Eli grinned in the dark. "Or... I might have just brought Daniel's great-uncle home."

Christina lifted her head, her eyes meeting his in the dim light. She leaned in, kissed him gently, and whispered, "Goodnight, Eli."

Then she turned out the lamp.

Chapter 20 - Christmas with the Kinds

The next day was Christmas Eve, but it began like any other on the Kind ranch. Christina was already in the kitchen, preparing breakfast, while Eli tended to the livestock. Normally, Daniel would be up helping, especially since he had school, but with no lessons today, Eli let him sleep in—he had more than earned it.

Whitey, however, was already awake and dressed by the time Eli stirred. As soon as he heard movement in the house, he was by the door, bundling up to head outside.

"Good morning," Christina greeted him with a warm smile. "Would you like some coffee before you go out?"

Whitey gave a slight nod. "Thank you, ma'am, but I'd best get to work."

Christina watched as he followed Eli out the door. The man hardly spoke, but his actions said plenty.

The ranch sparkled under a fresh coat of snow, the frost-covered trees glistening in the early morning light. The sky was clear and bright blue, a welcome change from the storm they had just endured.

After finishing the chores and clearing some snow from the mangers, Eli took a moment to point out some of the surrounding landmarks.

Standing behind the barn, he gestured toward the north. "That's Lookout Mountain. That's where Louis Thoen found the stone. When the weather clears, I'll take you up there so you can see it—and meet Louis."

Whitey nodded but remained quiet.

Eli continued, hoping that pointing out the land might trigger some memory. "That double-humped peak to the left is Crow Peak. I used to think it got its name because it kind of looks like a crow in flight, but I've heard there was a battle there between the Crow and Lakota."

At this, Whitey's eyes sharpened. He stared at the peak, tilting his head slightly.

"That is called Paha Karitukateyapi," Whitey said, his voice more certain than usual. "It means *The Hill Where the Crows Were Killed.* The Lakota fought a great battle there and drove the Crow from these lands."

Eli's stomach tightened. This was something new. Something he remembered.

"How do you know that?" Eli asked carefully.

Whitey's gaze remained on the peak. "When I first lived with the Lakota, they spoke of it often. It must have been many years ago, as no one in the village had been part of it. But I've seen this land before—we moved all across this valley."

Eli held his breath. Was this a real memory surfacing? Or was he simply repeating stories he had been told?

Whitey then turned, pointing southwest. "That mountain over there is Paha Sapa Paha—*Black Hills Mountain*. Spearfish itself was called Hočhápȟe."

The excitement in Eli's chest dimmed. Whitey was knowledgeable, but he was still reciting history, not remembering his own past.

Deciding not to push further, Eli clapped his gloved hands together. "Let's get inside. Christina's sure to have breakfast ready."

Whitey nodded, and they headed back toward the house.

As soon as they stepped inside, the scent of buttermilk pancakes filled the air.

At the kitchen table, Daniel was already digging into a stack of them. He looked up mid-bite. "Thanks for letting me sleep in, Dad!"

Eli grinned. "That's your reward for keeping up the place while I was gone. Maybe it's your Christmas present, too."

Daniel's eyes widened. "Oh no, I didn't ask for that! I'll trade my pancakes for something better!"

"I was just kidding," Eli chuckled. "I spoke to Santa—he says you're still on the *good* list. But I might take those pancakes anyway." He ruffled Daniel's hair on his way to kiss Christina on the cheek.

She smiled but nodded toward the counter. "I assume you saw the roast?"

"I did," Eli said. "That for tonight?"

"Yes," Christina replied. "I need someone to fetch apples, potatoes, and carrots from the cellar."

Daniel shot his hand up. "I'll do it! Can I get a second ask from Santa?" He smiled at his father.

Eli raised an eyebrow. "Not sure if that counts as *being good* or *blackmail*."

For the first time, Whitey surprised them all by joining in. "I think it makes him a good negotiator."

Everyone laughed. Christina handed plates of pancakes to Eli and Whitey before sitting down to join them.

As they ate, Christina turned to Whitey. "You'll meet more of the family this evening—James and Catherine Anderson."

Whitey looked up from his plate, his blue eyes meeting hers.

"We have a tradition of getting together for a meal and sharing stories on Christmas Eve," she continued.

"And presents from Grandma and Grandpa!" Daniel added enthusiastically.

Christina laughed. "Yes, that too."

As breakfast continued, they filled Whitey in on the Anderson family and how the ranch had evolved over the years.

The day passed quickly.

Eli and Whitey spent the afternoon clearing snowdrifts from the fences and driveway, ensuring that the Andersons could reach the house that evening.

Daniel fulfilled his mother's list from the cellar, then busied himself preparing the dining room—carefully setting out plates, candles, and festive decorations.

Christina stayed busy in the kitchen but took a break to call her parents, filling them in on Whitey's arrival before they made their way over.

James and Catherine Anderson's Road cart pulled by their black horse, Blackie, appeared in the snowy driveway just as dusk settled in. Daniel, watching from the dining room window, ran out without a coat to greet them.

Catherine barely had time to climb down before Daniel threw himself into her arms. "Daniel! Have you lost your mind? You'll catch your death running out here like this!" she scolded.

Daniel just grinned. "But Grandma, you'll keep me warm! Do you see our Christmas tree? I wanted you to see it from outside."

Catherine softened and gave him a squeeze. "It's beautiful. Did you help decorate?"

"Yes! Mom and I finished today, but Dad and I cut it last week."

By then, they had reached the house, and James called out, "You two get inside where it's warm. I'll tend to the cart."

Daniel hesitated. "I can help you, Grandpa."

James gave him a stern but kind look. "No, you help your grandmother inside and make sure she doesn't slip on the ice."

Inside, the warm glow of the fireplace and the delicious smell of roast beef greeted them. James led a short prayer, and soon the table was filled with laughter, conversation, and passing dishes.

Eli watched with satisfaction as Whitey settled in, listening intently to James's talk about his dairy business. Before long, Whitey was engaged in conversation, and by the time coffee and cookies were served, James had Whitey agreeing to help with the milking and delivery to Deadwood after Christmas.

As the evening wound down, Daniel grew increasingly restless. Christina noticed and leaned over. "What's wrong, sweetheart?" she asked softly.

Daniel whispered, "Will Santa skip our house if we're still awake?"

Christina smiled. "Oh no, sweetheart. He's watching and knows when it's time."

Daniel stole a glance at Whitey, then leaned closer and whispered, "Could Whitey be Santa Claus?"

Christina nearly burst out laughing but managed to keep a straight face. "No, but I can see why you'd think that."

She made a mental note to tell Eli later—it was too good not to share.

Sensing Daniel's worry, Christina helped bring the evening to a close, and soon, the Kind ranch was quiet once more, wrapped in the peaceful stillness of a Christmas Eve night.

Christmas morning couldn't come fast enough for Daniel. He bounded down the stairs and went straight to the fireplace, his eyes lighting up at the sight of the stockings. There were presents for everyone—including a stocking for Whitey.

Hearing movement in the kitchen, Daniel hesitated. He thought he was the first one up. Curious, he tiptoed over and peeked inside. In the dim light, he spotted Whitey sitting at the table, sipping a cup of coffee in silence. The sight startled him, but he managed to recover and said, "Good morning."

Whitey raised his cup slightly and mumbled, "Mornin'."

Just then, the kitchen lamp flicked on, and Christina appeared in her housecoat. "What are you two doing in the dark?" she asked, surprised.

Daniel quickly responded, "I just got here! I was checking if Santa had been here." He shot a sideways glance at Whitey, recalling their conversation the night before.

"Well, was he?" Christina asked with a knowing smile.

"Yes, he was!" Daniel confirmed, still eyeing Whitey with curiosity.

Whitey turned toward Christina. "I hope I didn't startle you, ma'am," he said. "I saw some leftover coffee in the pot from last night, so I heated it up."

"No problem at all," Christina replied warmly. "But let me make a fresh pot. I wouldn't mind some myself, and I'm sure Eli will be joining us soon."

A familiar voice called from the bedroom. "Sooner rather than later." Eli emerged, pulling on his suspenders with a stretch. "How

126

could I sleep with all this ruckus going on?" He grinned. "Merry Christmas, everyone."

Daniel and Christina echoed the greeting, while Whitey gave his usual grunt of acknowledgment.

Eli made his way to the door but stopped to give Christina a quick kiss on the cheek. Before he could bundle up, Daniel piped up excitedly. "Can we open presents now, or do we have to do chores first?"

Christina folded her arms and gave him a pointed look. "Daniel, I think you know the answer to that."

Daniel sighed dramatically as he grabbed his coat. "I know, but I thought maybe—just maybe—someone might be more excited than me to see what's in the stockings." He cast another quick glance at Whitey.

Whitey caught his eye and, to Daniel's surprise, grinned. "I'm excited too," he said, standing. "So, I'll help with chores. That way, we can get back here faster."

Daniel's face lit up, and with that, the three of them bundled up and headed outside.

The chores went quickly, helped by the relatively mild weather. As Eli and Whitey hauled hay for the horses, Eli turned to him.

"I think we should head into Spearfish soon to see the Thoen Stone. The trail will be a lot easier in this weather." He grimaced, recalling their treacherous journey through the blizzard.

Whitey nodded and smiled, but before he could reply, Daniel's voice rang out from the barn. "Hurry up, you two! I'm done with my chores, and I'm ready for presents!"

The three met at the front door, with Daniel leading the charge inside. Christina was waiting, a warm breakfast of biscuits and bacon already on the table. She knew that breakfast would be nothing more than a brief intermission between Daniel and his presents.

Before long, the dining room was filled with the sound of tearing paper. Most gifts were wrapped in plain brown kraft paper, while a few were in newspaper. The special ones, wrapped in green paper, caught Whitey's eye. He picked up a scrap and studied it. "I've never seen wrapping paper like this before," he mused.

Daniel had saved his green-wrapped present for last, knowing it was something special. He tore open the others first—a new pair of jeans, warm socks, and mittens. Christina noticed a flicker of disappointment in his eyes as he unwrapped a nice dress shirt. She placed a hand on his shoulder. "Santa must've known how much you grew this year and how much you needed new clothes."

Daniel mustered a smile, but his eyes quickly darted to the last, long green package sitting by his stocking. Just as he reached for it, Eli held up a hand.

"Hold on there, mister." He finished off his biscuit and leaned back in his chair. "Where are your manners? Shouldn't we all get to finish opening our presents first?"

Daniel groaned, setting the package down. "Sorry," he mumbled, slumping into his chair.

Eli glared. "Let's see... Santa brought your mother a beautiful tablecloth and a picture frame. Whitey got some jerky and a pair of gloves. And I got new pliers and gloves myself."

Daniel fidgeted, clearly impatient. As soon as Eli finished, he perked up. "Now is it my turn?"

At Eli and Christina's nod, Daniel snatched up the green package and ripped off the paper. His face split into a grin as he let out a victorious "Yes!"

In his hands was a brand-new Stevens Favorite rifle. He carefully pulled it free from the green paper, then raised it to his shoulder, aiming as if he were shooting out the window. The rest of the gifts instantly faded in importance. He turned to Eli, eyes shining. "Now I can go hunting with you—with my own gun!"

Eli smiled. "That's the plan."

Christina, watching from across the table, crossed her arms. "You need to be careful with that."

"I know, Mom," Daniel said earnestly. "Dad taught me well with Opa's gun." He pointed to the Sharps rifle hanging above the door.

Whitey followed Daniel's gaze and nodded toward the rifle. "That's a Sharps, right?"

Eli nodded. "Yes, it was my father's rifle. The first gun he ever bought new—and the first one I ever shot." He glanced at Whitey, curious about his interest. "My uncle Richard sent it to me on my wedding day."

Eli saw an opportunity. "My father passed when I was in the Army at Fort Abraham Lincoln—right after the Black Hills Expedition. By the time I got home, my mother had passed too. My sister, Emily, and I buried them at the family farm. We weren't sure what to do with it, and my uncle Richard, my father's youngest brother, had just come to America. He ended up taking over the farm."

Eli watched Whitey closely, hoping something might stir in him—some recognition, some memory. But Whitey simply asked, "It's a .44?"

Before Eli could push further, Daniel's excited voice broke in. "Can we go shooting, Dad?"

Eli turned back to Whitey, nodding. "Yes, it's a .44." Then he looked at Daniel. "Sure, but you'll need to help your mother clear the table first."

The rest of the morning was spent outside, testing out the new rifle. Whitey proved to be an excellent marksman and even offered Daniel some pointers. Christina joined in, surprising everyone with her accuracy.

That afternoon, the Andersons arrived again, bringing a cured ham for supper. Daniel proudly showed off his rifle, and the evening passed quickly with storytelling and games.

Later that night, as Eli and Christina lay in bed, Christina sighed. "I wish I could see Whitey without that thick beard."

Eli chuckled. "Why?"

"I just want to see the face behind those eyes."

Eli was silent for a moment. Then he admitted, "You know, it might sound strange, but I see my father's eyes in him."

Christina turned toward him. "Even stranger... I see you in his eyes."

Eli exhaled. "Maybe we're just seeing what we want to see."

"Maybe," Christina said. "Or maybe we're finally seeing the truth."

Chapter 21- A Visit to The Anderson Ranch

The next morning began like any other on the Kind ranch. Dawn brought the familiar rhythm—Eli and Daniel tending to the livestock while Christina prepared a hearty breakfast. Whitey had fallen into the routine as well, already up before sunrise and brewing coffee in the dim kitchen. Daniel, enjoying his time off from school, was eager to help his father with whatever tasks the day had in store.

As they gathered around the breakfast table, Eli laid out the plan. Turning to Daniel, he said, "I'd like to walk the fence line today, check for snow drifts that the livestock could walk over. Think you can give me a hand?"

Daniel, chewing on a piece of jerky, lit up. "Sure, Dad! Can I bring my gun?"

Eli grinned. "We'll do some shooting later. We'll be carrying shovels, and that's enough weight to haul around for now."

Daniel's enthusiasm dimmed slightly, but he nodded. "Okay."

Eli then turned to Whitey. "I heard you and James talking about the Anderson ranch last night. It'd be a good day to go see the operation while Daniel and I check fences. We'll meet you over there when we're done."

Whitey took a sip of coffee and gave a slight nod of agreement.

Eli continued, "Their ranch is just east of here, on the other side of Elk Mountain. I know James told you to follow the trail, but by now, there are probably more paths than just one. I'll point out the valley you'll ride through—once you're in it, you won't miss the Milk Road leading straight to the Anderson ranch."

Christina poured more coffee into Whitey's cup and added, "My parents are looking forward to showing you around."

Daniel grinned as he finished the last of his bacon. "I bet Grandma has cookies for you!"

A rare smile crossed Whitey's face. "I want to thank you all for taking me in like this. I could get used to this family thing."

Christina set the coffeepot down and met his gaze. "We're happy to have you here, Whitey. We want you to feel like family."

Eli watched closely for any reaction from Whitey, wondering if the word "family" stirred anything in him. But Whitey remained unreadable.

Eli and Daniel helped Whitey tack up his horse, pointing him in the right direction toward the Anderson ranch.

"We'll join you later," Eli called out as Whitey trotted down the driveway. Whitey raised a hand in acknowledgment before spurring his horse into a gallop.

Eli and Daniel spent the morning walking the fence line, finding a few places where snowdrifts had piled high enough for the livestock to climb over. Only one spot required serious shoveling; the rest could be packed down. By midday, their job was done, and soon they were saddled up, riding toward the Anderson ranch.

When they arrived, they spotted Whitey helping James load milk onto the wagon.

Eli swung down from his horse and grinned. "I see James already put you to work."

Whitey nodded as he hefted a cream can onto the wagon.

James chuckled. "Whitey got here just in time for the last milking shift. He's been a great help—I might have to send a letter to Teddy Roosevelt and see about stealing him away."

Eli laughed. "I figured as much. I suppose you'd like him to ride along to Deadwood with this load, too?"

"If he's willing," James said, glancing at Whitey.

Whitey finished loading a cream can and nodded. "I'm impressed with what you've built here, James. Especially the spring house—having running water that doesn't freeze in winter and stays cool in summer is smart. There's a lot more to a milking operation than I ever knew. I'd like to ride along to Deadwood; I've never been there."

James climbed onto the wagon's buckboard and gestured to the empty seat beside him. "I'll have him back before dark—and promise not to spend too much time at the gambling tables." He smiled and gave the reins a flick.

Whitey climbed up beside him, and with a soft cluck of his tongue, James urged the horses forward.

The Anderson Ranch

Eli turned to Daniel. "You'd better run up to the house and say hello to Grandma before we head back."

Daniel didn't need to be told twice. He sprinted up the steps and disappeared inside while Eli led the horses around to the front.

A moment later, Daniel emerged with cookies in hand, his grandmother trailing behind.

Eli waved and called out, "Thanks for spoiling us!"

"Always," Catherine replied with a laugh. "I never miss a chance to spoil my boys."

"Thanks, Grandma!" Daniel called as he swung onto Buster, carefully balancing his cookies. "See you again soon!"

Eli and Daniel spent the rest of the afternoon handling ranch chores, then took some time to practice shooting with Daniel's new rifle. As dusk settled over the ranch, Whitey rode in just in time for supper.

Eli grinned. "Good timing. Christina just rang the supper bell."

Daniel scrunched up his nose. "I didn't hear a bell—just Mom yelling for us to get inside before our food got cold."

Eli chuckled. "It's just a figure of speech." Then he paused. "But that does give me an idea."

The supper conversation revolved around Whitey's trip to Deadwood. Predictably, he didn't say much, but he did share that the town wasn't a place he'd want to visit often. He also mentioned that he ran into Sheriff Bullock again.

Eli perked up. "Did he remember you?"

"How could you forget this face?" Whitey said dryly.

The whole table laughed.

Eli, still mulling over how to introduce Whitey to the Thoen Stone, decided to take a different approach.

"I was thinking after chores tomorrow, we could take a trip into Spearfish and check out the spot they're considering for the new fish hatchery."

Daniel looked up from where he was sprawled on the rug in front of the fire. "What's a fish hatchery?"

135

"I'm glad you asked," Eli said. "You know how we usually smoke sucker fish when we catch them? Well, they're talking about raising trout—fish we won't have to smoke before eating. A man named Hector Bayer from the U.S. Fish Commission is looking at a site behind the old John Johnson sawmill."

Whitey nodded but stayed quiet.

"I also need to pick up some grain and nails at Cashner's," Eli added. "And you know John Cashner—he'll have plenty of gossip about it. Unless, of course, someone would rather stay home and clean out the stalls?"

Daniel shot up from the floor. "Oh no, I'm going! In fact, I'm hitting the hay right now so I'll be ready!"

Laughter filled the room as they all agreed with Daniel and turned in for the night.

As Eli and Christina settled into bed, Eli turned to her. "Do you think I'm doing the right thing taking Whitey into Spearfish?"

Christina thought for a moment. "Just ask him straight up if he wants to see the stone. No trickery—just an honest question."

Eli sighed. "You're right. I was thinking of calling John Cashner to have the stone back in his store when we got there, but that would be sneaky."

Christina smiled. "No need for tricks. Just see if he wants to go."

Eli nodded and pulled the blankets up. "Tomorrow, we'll find out."

Chapter 22 – Spearfish (Almost)

B reakfast started with Eli following through on his promise to Christina by asking Whitey,

"Whitey, since we're going into Spearfish, would you like to see the real Thoen Stone? "Whitey looked up from his breakfast and simply said, "Sure," before returning to his plate.

Eli glanced at Christina, who gave him a knowing look that said, "See? That wasn't so hard."

With that settled, Eli turned his thoughts to whether Louis would be home. He doubted Louis would have gone anywhere so soon after Christmas, but he figured it wouldn't hurt to check. The Thoen's didn't have a phone, but Louis regularly stopped by Cashner Hardware for coffee. Since Eli needed to pick up supplies there anyway, he decided to call while Daniel and Whitey hitched up the buggy for the trip to Spearfish.

Just as Eli reached for the receiver, the phone rang. Startled, he lifted it off the hook and answered, "Hello?"

A familiar but panicked voice came through the speaker.

"Eli, this is Catherine. The Turgeon cattle have gotten in with our dairy herd, and James needs help—please! He doesn't think the bull is with them, but we're not sure yet."

"We're on our way," Eli assured her, quickly hanging up.

He ran outside to the waiting buggy. "Change of plans!" he announced. "The Turgeon herd got into the Anderson pasture and mixed with the dairy cows. Daniel, get Ginger and Buster saddled up."

Then, turning to Christina and Whitey, he added, "You two take the buggy, but go slow—the trail is muddy."

Whitey spoke up. "I'll bring my horse too. She's handy at cutting."

"Good idea," Eli agreed. Then, to Christina, "Take your time, and be careful. If you hear us coming, pull off the trail so we can pass without spooking your horse."

"I'll be fine," Christina reassured him with a smile. "I'll pull over if that makes you feel better."

Eli chuckled, blew her a kiss, and followed Daniel and Whitey into the barn to saddle up.

As they cinched their saddles, Eli filled Whitey in. "Ferdinand Turgeon's pasture borders the Andersons'. He usually doesn't have cattle out this time of year, so I'm wondering what happened."

Daniel chimed in, "Do you think they got over a snowdrift, Dad?"

"Could be," Eli nodded.

Daniel frowned. "We should've checked Grandpa's fences yesterday too."

"Yeah, I feel bad about that," Eli admitted. "But your grandpa usually keeps a close eye on things."

As they mounted up, Daniel asked Whitey, "What's your horse's name?"

Whitey looked at him and said, "Sun'ka Wakan."

Daniel tried to repeat the name in his head but didn't quite get it before Whitey galloped off after Eli.

The trio caught up to Christina just before she reached the Milk Road. True to her word, she pulled over when she heard them approaching. Eli blew her another kiss as they passed.

As they neared the Anderson ranch, they saw James and Catherine in the cattle lot, slipping around in the mud, trying to keep the herds apart.

Eli swung off his horse at the gate, leading it through while Daniel and Whitey followed on theirs.

Over the hooting and hollering, James shouted, "The damn bull's in here too—he's by the fence behind those heifers!" He pointed. "Eli, keep an eye on him. Daniel, Whitey—keep the herds apart while I get my horse."

James turned to Catherine and ordered, "Ma, get out of this mud before you get hurt!"

Relieved, Catherine shuffled through the muck toward the gate, where Christina helped her through.

The two herds settled slightly, and James soon returned on horseback. He rode up beside Eli.

"At least they're easy to tell apart," James grumbled. "I just don't want any Hereford crossing my Holsteins!"

Eli smirked. "That'd be a different color, for sure."

Daniel, still working the cattle, shouted, "Grandpa, how'd they get in?"

James sighed. "Not sure. I walked the fences yesterday, but we had wind. Maybe a drift was high enough—but I doubt it was solid enough to hold their weight. I noticed them when I went out for the second milking shift. They were drinking at the trough like they owned the place!"

James glanced toward the barn, spotting Catherine and Christina heading inside. He called out, " Catherine, can you give the cows in the stanchions some more grain so they don't get restless?"

She waved back in agreement, and the two women disappeared inside.

James turned back to Eli. "Let's ease that bull out first. Once he's gone, we'll let Daniel and Buster show us what they can do."

Daniel's face lit up. He straightened in the saddle, gripping the reins tighter.

Eli moved in on the horned Hereford bull, who stomped in the mud a few times before turning and trotting out of the lot. With the bull gone, it was Daniel's turn.

The Anderson dairy cows barely needed moving, but the Turgeon herd was feistier. Some kicked at the air, others turned sharply, testing Buster and Daniel. But they held their ground, and soon the last stray cow was through the gate.

James beamed. "Nice work, Daniel! You're turning into a fine horseman!"

Daniel blushed, patting Buster's neck. "Thanks, Grandpa!"

The next step was driving the cattle back and finding the breach. James rode ahead while Eli, Daniel, and Whitey herded the cattle along the muddy trail.

At the north end of the pasture, they saw the trail leading into a stand of cottonwoods—where a huge limb had crashed through the fence.

James had the fence opened up by the time Ferdinand Turgeon rode up.

Ferdinand shook his head. "Guess I should've checked my herd sooner."

Eli nodded. "Your water must've frozen over, so they wandered to the next best thing."

Ferdinand chuckled. "Guess yours tastes better." Then, turning serious, "Did Big Red cause any trouble, or do I need to watch for red-speckled Holsteins?"

James huffed, clearly unimpressed. "No, I caught him before he had the chance."

The five men worked together, clearing fallen branches and fixing the fence. Daniel and Whitey even stomped down the drifts, ensuring the cattle wouldn't escape again.

Afterward, Ferdinand offered lunch, but James declined, "I've got cows to finish milking—another time."

With the situation handled, the Kinds and Whitey made their way back. The pace was slower, and Daniel finally asked the question that had been nagging at him.

"Whitey, what did you call your horse again?"

Whitey shifted in his saddle and said, "Šúŋka Wakȟáŋ. It means 'sacred horse.'"

Daniel furrowed his brow. "So... you call your horse, 'horse'?"

Whitey chuckled. "Well, yes, in a way." Then, after a pause, he added, "By the way, Daniel, you handled Buster really well today. We all stood back and watched you cut those Herefords out like a pro. It was impressive."

Daniel ducked his head, a shy grin spreading across his face. "Thanks."

The rest of the day was spent giving extra care to the horses after their hard work. Daniel brushed Buster until every trace of mud was gone, his coat gleaming in the late afternoon sun.

As they finished up at the barn, Eli clapped Daniel on the shoulder as he was looking at Whitey too. "I know today didn't go as planned, but don't worry—our trip to Spearfish is still happening. Just a little delay, that's all."

Daniel nodded eagerly, his excitement renewed. "I can't wait!" Whitey only tilted his head in agreement.

Chapter 23 - Spearfish (Finally)

The next morning, the sun rose bright in the eastern sky, but Eli noticed dark clouds gathering to the west. He knew the weather was about to change again. "We need to finish chores quickly so we can get to Spearfish before we're delayed another day," he announced at breakfast.

Luckily, most of the buggy rigging had been left on from the day before, so it didn't take long for Eli, Whitey, and Daniel to get it ready. Eli tossed a couple of blankets into the back. "I don't trust this weather. I think we're in for a change again," he said. "Daniel, can you lead Blackie and the buggy out front? I need to call John Cashner to let him know we're coming."

Eli picked up the receiver and cranked the phone, half expecting to be interrupted again. The familiar voice of Kate answered, cheerful as always. "Who would you like to speak with?"

"Hello, Kate. I'd like to speak with John Cashner, please."

"Certainly, Eli. I'll connect you now," she replied.

After a few seconds of buzzing in his ear, John's voice came through. "Cashner Hardware. How can I help you?"

"Hi, John, it's Eli Kind."

"Well, hello, Eli!" John replied. "Good to hear from you. Last time I saw you, I was worried you wouldn't make it home in that blizzard, but Kate said you called Tom in Belle that night, so I knew you were safe. What can I do for you?"

"I'm coming to town today. I need six fifty-pound bags of oats, ten pounds of wire nails, and five pounds of horseshoe nails."

"That's all?" John asked, surprised.

"For now," Eli chuckled. "Also, did Louis bring his stone back to your store?"

"Not yet," John said. "But I did mention you stopped by the other day looking for it so I will mention it again as I am sure he will be by for coffee today"

"Just let him know I'll be in town with my friend Whitey." Eli said —"the man you met the other day. I'd like to show him the stone."

"Will do, Eli. I'll see you later today."

"Thanks, John," Eli said, hanging up the phone. He dashed outside to the waiting buggy, where everyone was already seated and ready to go.

Climbing aboard, Eli grabbed the reins from Daniel. "We'll head to the hardware store first, then over to the Thoen's. We'll check out the hatchery site on the way home."

With no objections from the others, the buggy rolled down the driveway toward Spearfish. As they traveled, Eli pointed out landmarks. "That's the shortcut Whitey and I took in the blizzard. Good thing I ran into the railroad mile marker over there, or we might not have found our way home."

Daniel's eyes widened. "Was it really that bad? You couldn't even see the house from here?"

"It was that bad," Eli confirmed, glancing at Whitey, who gave a slow nod. "Luckily, the train had already passed, clearing the track enough for us to follow. I was just hoping it wouldn't come back while we were on it!"

Christina cut in. "I hope you learned a lesson from that, Mr. Kind."

"I did," Eli said with a grin. "Always check the train schedule before using the tracks as a road."

"That's not what I meant, and you know it," Christina scolded, shaking her head. The rest of the group chuckled.

The trip to town didn't take long, and as they pulled up to Cashner Hardware, they saw several bags and boxes stacked neatly on the porch.

John stepped outside just as Eli helped Christina down from the buggy. "Well, well, if it isn't the whole Kind crew!" he called out. "I've got your order ready, but come on in—I've got fresh coffee, and Louis is here."

As they filed inside, John shook Whitey's hand. "Pleasure to meet you again, Whitey. At least this time, the weather's better."

Eli, already inside, overheard and turned back with a grin. "For now, but I've got a feeling it's going to change soon."

John nodded. "I feel it too. Help yourself to coffee—I need to check on an order out back, but I'll be right back."

The group gathered around the potbellied stove in the middle of the store, where Louis Thoen sat in a rocking chair, coffee in hand. He raised his cup. "Well, hello to the Kind family! Merry late Christmas and an early Happy New Year to you all."

"Same to you, Louis," Eli said, then gestured toward Whitey. "This is my friend Whitey. Whitey, this is Louis Thoen—the man who found the stone I told you about."

Louis stood and shook Whitey's hand. "Pleasure to meet you."

Whitey nodded, then took a seat by the stove.

Louis motioned toward the coffee pot. "Help yourself—fresh brew."

Eli shook his head. "Thanks, but I had my fill before we left home." Christina and Whitey declined as well, Christina with a polite "No, thank you," and Whitey with a low grunt.

Louis sipped his coffee. "What brings you to town today, Eli?"

Eli leaned back in his chair. "We needed some supplies, but I was hoping to show Whitey the stone. John said you took it back home?"

"I did," Louis said, "but when John mentioned you might be coming, I put it back in the store window." He pointed across the room.

"Oh, I missed it coming in," Eli said, walking over to retrieve the stone.

"I'm working on making copies to take to Rapid City—see if anyone recognizes it," Louis explained as Eli handed the stone to Whitey.

Thoen Stone

Whitey turned it over carefully, tracing the carved letters with his fingers. Eli watched closely, resisting the urge to ask questions. Christina, sensing his anticipation, leaned in as well.

Louis spoke up. "Be careful not to rub on the letters. The sandstone is delicate—it doesn't take much to wear it down."

Whitey pulled his hand back. "Sorry. I didn't mean to damage it." He paused, studying the stone. "Where did you find this?"

Louis took the stone back and wrapped it in cloth. "Just up the hill on Lookout Mountain. If we step outside, I can point it out."

Everyone except John followed Louis onto the porch. He pointed to a ravine. "See that small oak tree? Just to the right of it—that's where I found it. Might've washed down from farther up over the years. I'd take you up there, but with all this snow, it'd be quite the hike."

Whitey stood silently, staring at the mountain. Snowflakes swirled in the wind as the air turned colder.

Louis clapped his hands together. "It's warmer inside by the stove if you have more questions."

Eli hesitated, glancing at Whitey before agreeing. "Not today. We'll come back when the weather's better."

As the others turned to head inside, Christina whispered to Eli, "Do you think he's remembering something?"

"I hope so," Eli said.

Daniel had just reached the porch when Eli called out. "Daniel, let's load our supplies before we go in to warm up."

It didn't take them more than a few minutes to get everything secured before they quickly made their way inside to the warmth of the wood stove.

Inside, as they gathered around the stove, Louis leaned back in his chair and asked, "So, Whitey, what do you think? Do you believe my stone is real?"

Whitey rubbed his hands in front of the stove. "It seems like a tragic event. I'm not sure what to think, but I can see why Eli would want to know more—for his family's sake. Are there any other names tied to it around here?"

Louis glanced at Eli and said, "Besides the woman Eli found, the one who claimed she was married to the DeLacompt fellow named on the stone, most of what we have are just rumors. I still need to follow up on the story about some deserters from Captain Bonneville's party a few years before the stone's date."

Eli perked up. "I hadn't heard that one, Louis."

Louis opened the stove door, added another log to the fire, and, as he closed it, said, "I ran into a fellow named Frank Thomson. He told me he'd read a journal from Bonneville's expedition, and some of the names in it matched the ones on the stone."

Eli's curiosity sharpened. "Could I meet this Mr. Thomson sometime? I'd like to hear what he knows."

"Of course," Louis replied. "I'll let you know next time he's in town."

Eli turned toward Whitey, who had settled into a chair and was staring into the flames, lost in thought.

"You alright?" Eli asked.

Whitey slowly looked up. "Yeah, sorry. Just thinking."

Eli glanced out the large hardware store window, watching the snow come down harder now. "I think we'd better head home before we end up in another adventure like the one Whitey and I had a few days ago."

John Cashner, who had joined them as Louis talked about Captain Bonneville, nodded. "I've met Mr. Thomson, and I think he's onto something, Eli. But I also agree—you should head home now so I don't have to sit by the party line listening to make sure you make it back safely."

Christina smiled warmly. "We'll call you directly when we get home, John. And thank you for caring about us."

Eli grinned. "Yes, we promise to call as soon as we're back. But before we go, I wanted to ask—what's the latest on the rumors about the fish hatchery? Is that even the right term for it?"

John grimaced. "Oh, so now I'm the town's official rumor mill?"

Everyone laughed—except Whitey, who was still deep in thought, staring into the fire.

John continued, "What I've heard is that we have the perfect streams and climate for raising trout. Mr. Evermann from the U.S. Fish Commission came through recently, scouting locations. Word is, they've chosen Ames Canyon, where John Johnson's sawmill sits. I figure that's true because Johnson was in here buying supplies for gold panning. He's planning to head up to the Klondike Gold Rush in Alaska."

Eli raised an eyebrow. "There's still gold in these hills—why is he going all the way to Alaska to look for it?"

John shrugged. "I don't know, but he must have gotten a good offer on his place."

Just then, Whitey, who had been silent, suddenly blurted out, "Did anyone ever find the gold from the stone?"

The unexpected outburst took everyone by surprise. Louis was the first to respond. "Not yet, Whitey, but not for lack of trying. Ever since I found the stone and word got out, hardly a day passes without someone poking around the quarry looking for it."

Whitey absorbed the answer, then abruptly stood and walked toward the door.

Eli, sensing Whitey's unease, felt a little embarrassed by his abrupt exit. He quickly thanked everyone and wished them a Happy New Year before following Whitey outside into the snowy afternoon.

Back in the buggy, Christina pulled her coat tighter. "Daniel, pass me a blanket."

Eli, adjusting the reins, added, "Might as well pull them all out. I want to swing by Ames Canyon really quick and see if anything's happening with the hatchery."

Bundled up against the cold, they made their way into the canyon. As they entered, the wind eased, and the snowfall lightened. The towering canyon walls, still wet from earlier melting snow, were now beginning to glaze over with ice.

Christina admired the scene. "This is such a beautiful place. It would make a great location for a hatchery, much better than an abandoned sawmill."

Eli nodded. "Looks like Johnson has already left. This is a perfect spot—good water, and the stream runs right through it." He pointed to the icy creek below. "See how this creek freezes from the bottom up?"

Daniel peered down. "I never noticed that before. Why does it do that?"

Christina chimed in. "Grandpa Anderson always said Spearfish Creek runs too fast for the ice to form properly on the top."

Daniel thought for a moment. "Do you think the new fish will like that?"

His mother laughed. "I guess we'll find out."

Eli turned the buggy around and headed home. The wind picked up again, but the snowfall remained light.

Back at the ranch, chores were finished just as the sun dipped below the horizon. Whitey had barely spoken since leaving the hardware store, which worried Eli.

Christina had supper waiting, and though the evening conversation revolved around the day's events, Whitey remained unusually quiet.

Later, as everyone gathered by the fire, Eli finally broke the silence. "Did something happen today that upset you?"

Whitey took a deep breath, staring into the flames. "I have so many thoughts and questions running through my head, I don't even know where to start."

Eli hesitated. "I'd like to help if you want to talk about it."

Whitey remained silent for a long moment, then finally said, "I think I'll turn in for the night."

"Alright," Eli said softly. "Goodnight."

Whitey gave his usual grunt in reply and disappeared up the stairs.

Once they heard his door close, Christina glanced at Daniel, who was playing a game of solitaire at the table. "Are you ready for bed?"

"Can I finish this game? I think I might win this time."

"Sure," Christina said as she tidied up around the room.

A few minutes later, Daniel let out a disappointed sigh. "Dang, I was so close—just a few cards left."

Eli chuckled. "You can try again tomorrow."

Daniel put away his cards and called out, "Goodnight!" as he headed upstairs.

Finally, Eli and Christina had a quiet moment to themselves.

They both knew Whitey was struggling with something, but neither of them knew how to help.

"Maybe he just needs time," Christina said.

Eli sighed. "I hope so. I just hope, when he's ready, we can help him find the answers he's looking for."

Chapter 24 - Whitey's Departure?

The next morning at breakfast, Whitey told the Kinds that he planned to return to the Elkhorn Ranch.

It wasn't a surprise to Eli and Christina. They had discussed it the night before—despite Whitey being a man of few words, he seemed restless, as if he didn't fully belong. Eli had hoped that seeing the Thoen Stone would stir something in him, unlocking a connection to the past, but instead, Whitey had only withdrawn further. Maybe Eli was chasing a ghost, seeing patterns where none existed. Still, how could so many clues point to Whitey, yet he remembered nothing?

Eli felt a growing need to address it but didn't want Daniel involved in something he couldn't fully understand. Looking for an excuse to send him away, he said, "Daniel, could you check the water tank? Make sure the hole's still open for the livestock."

Daniel, already half-dressed for the cold, nodded and dashed outside.

As soon as the door shut, Eli looked across the table at Whitey. "Whitey, we don't want you to go," he said earnestly. "We had hoped showing you the Thoen Stone and where it was found might trigger something. But whether it does or not, you're family. If you feel you need to leave, we won't stop you—but I don't have a good feeling about the weather. Maybe stay a little longer?"

Christina added, "I agree with Eli. Daniel loves having you here—I think he sees you as his roommate upstairs."

Whitey rolled his coffee cup between his hands, staring into it as if looking for answers. Then he looked up, seeing Daniel making his way back to the house, and said, "I appreciate everything you've done for me. This is the closest I've felt to being part of a family since I left the tribes. I should be heading back—but let's see what the weather does tomorrow."

Eli and Christina exchanged glances before nodding in agreement.

Daniel burst through the door, cheeks red from the cold. "The cows must've been real thirsty—they kept the hole open all night. I topped off the tank."

"Thanks, Daniel," Eli said, though he knew he had already done it earlier.

The rest of the day passed as usual, but Eli noticed Whitey spending more time with Daniel, the two laughing and joking as they worked.

That evening, Eli and Christina sat by the fire, talking.

"I know you're disappointed," Christina said gently. "Finding Whitey felt like a miracle, and I know you hoped he'd help solve the mystery of your uncle. But even if we don't have answers yet, we've gained a good friend. And maybe what we've learned will matter someday."

Eli sighed. "I really wanted to take him to the spot where Louis found the stone."

"We still can," Christina reassured him. "Maybe in the spring, after calving season. The Hills are beautiful then—hard to forget."

Eli nodded. "I'll ask him in the morning."

155

Morning came with a sharp chill. Before Eli even got out of bed, he muttered, "It dropped overnight. I'll get the stove going."

As he stepped out of the bedroom, he heard the familiar crackle of firewood. To his surprise, Whitey was already at the kitchen table, sitting in the dim light, staring into his coffee.

"Morning," Eli said.

"Morning," Whitey mumbled. "Thought I'd get an early start."

Eli hesitated. He still hoped Whitey might stay. "Appreciate you getting the stove going. It's colder than it's been."

Whitey nodded toward the window. "Still too dark to see the western sky."

"Let's warm up and have some coffee," Eli suggested.

Whitey poured them both a cup, and as Christina entered, she smiled. "I see you boys have things started. Guess I'd better make breakfast."

"I already told him we'll miss him," Eli said with a smirk.

Christina laughed. "Then I won't stroke his ego again."

For a moment, they thought they saw a small smile under Whitey's beard.

By the time it was light enough to see outside, snowflakes were swirling, and the wind howled through the house.

"You sure about leaving today?" Eli asked.

Whitey studied the storm outside. "I'll help with chores—see what it looks like after that."

"And after breakfast," Christina insisted, placing biscuits on the table.

Whitey gave his usual nod, a sign he agreed.

Outside, the wind cut through their coats like a knife. Snow whipped sideways, making it hard to tell if more was falling or if the wind was simply stirring up what had already fallen. Eli knew one thing for certain—traveling in this would be dangerous.

As they finished up chores, Daniel came running into the barn, breathless.

"Daniel, what are you doing out here dressed like that?" Eli scolded.

"I came to say goodbye to Whitey," Daniel panted, "but the phone rang—Mom said it's Dr. M. He needs to talk to you right away!"

Eli tensed. "Alright. Get back inside before you freeze."

Whitey watched silently as Eli hurried after Daniel.

Eli barely had time to take off his gloves before grabbing the phone. Christina was still on the line. "Here he is, Doctor. Take care— I hope to see you again soon."

She handed the receiver to Eli, her expression tight with concern.

"Hello, Dr. M. It's been a while."

Dr. Valentine McGillycuddy's voice came through the line. "Eli, I wish I were calling under better circumstances."

"What's wrong?"

"There was a battle yesterday at Pine Ridge Agency," Dr. M said grimly. "I don't have all the details yet—just that there are heavy casualties, and there may still be fighting. I need help."

Eli didn't hesitate. "You know I'll help, but this storm—"

"I understand. That's why I'm arranging for you to take the train from Whitewood to Rapid City. From there, we'll take it to Buffalo Gap, where the Army has a stage waiting."

"That's better than traveling by horseback. What should I prepare for?"

A long pause. Then Dr. M's voice came quieter. "A lot of death." He sighed. "Bring your sidearm and rifle. I hope we won't need them. The Army will provide the rest. Be prepared to work with the tribes."

Eli's stomach twisted. "Which tribes?"

"Mostly Lakota Sioux."

Silence hung between them.

"You still there, Eli?"

Eli shook himself from his thoughts. "Yes. I'll be there. Can I bring someone along?"

"Of course. Do I know him?"

"Not really. I'll ask him first and call you back."

As Eli hung up, he turned to find Christina and Daniel watching him.

Daniel, always eager, blurted, "If you're gonna ask me to go, the answer's yes!"

Christina shot him a sharp look. "The answer is no." She turned to Eli. "You're thinking about Whitey, aren't you? Do you think that's wise? You'd be asking him to go to a place where soldiers just killed people from the tribe that raised him."

Eli ran a hand through his hair. "He could be a huge help— translating, explaining tribal customs—but I see your point."

At that moment, the door opened. Whitey stepped inside, his coat dusted with snow. He saw their expressions and frowned.

Eli squared his shoulders. "Whitey, let's sit down. I need to talk to you."

They gathered at the table.

"I just got a call from my friend Dr. M," Eli explained. "There was a battle at Pine Ridge. He doesn't know the details, but it sounds bad. He's asking for help, and I'm going."

Whitey sat up. "What do you mean, 'battle'?"

"Lakota Sioux were involved."

Whitey stood abruptly. "I'll go."

Eli blinked. "Just like that?"

Whitey nodded. "I was leaving anyway."

Eli hesitated, then said, "We're taking the train from Whitewood. We'll need Christina and Daniel to take us to the depot."

Whitey didn't hesitate. "I'll be ready."

Eli turned to Christina. "I'll call Dr. M back. We leave today."

It was nearly 9:30 by the time Eli and Whitey, with Daniel's help, had the buggy hitched and ready to go. Christina joined them, handing Eli a basket filled with food for the journey.

The wind cut through their layers as they settled under heavy blankets, bracing against the bitter cold. Daniel burrowed his head beneath the covers whenever a strong gust pelted them with icy snow. What should have been a quick 20-minute ride to the Whitewood depot felt much longer in the harsh weather.

Upon arriving, Eli convinced Christina that he and Daniel should head straight back before conditions worsened. He reassured her that he would call as soon as they arrived in Rapid City, kissed her goodbye, and sent her and Daniel off into the blinding snow.

Inside the depot, the waiting area was packed. Normally, travelers would linger on the platform, but today, everyone huddled indoors to escape the cold. Men in wool suits and women in long dresses with bonnets stood shoulder to shoulder, filling the space. Eli, dressed in his best suit, glanced at Whitey, who was wearing Eli's second-best. Though a bit loose, it gave him a respectable appearance.

Eli made his way to the ticket counter, where he spotted an envelope with his name next to the telegraph machine. He gestured toward it. "I believe those are my tickets over there?"

The ticket clerk looked up and smiled. "Yes, Mr. Kind, they were called in earlier today by Dr. McGillycuddy."

Eli blinked, then grinned. "Ben! I didn't recognize you with that hat on—sorry about that."

"No problem, Mr. Kind. I get that all the time," Ben said with a chuckle, handing him the tickets. "Have a good trip, and try to stay warm!"

"Thanks, Ben," Eli replied, turning to hand Whitey his ticket.

Just then, the crisp voices of uniformed conductors called out, "All aboard!" Steam hissed from the black locomotive as it prepared for departure, the thickening snowfall making the gold-leaf lettering of *Chicago, Burlington & Quincy* on the tender barely visible. Even in the storm, Eli could make out freight yard workers still loading the cargo cars as he and Whitey stepped aboard.

A ticket usher directed them to their seats in the first-class coach. As they moved through the car, Eli noticed the plush, padded seats and turned to Whitey with a smirk. "Looks like the good doctor booked us first class. I've never traveled like this before, but I sure hope they intend to warm it up in here."

As he slid into a seat, Eli hesitated and then gestured toward the window. "The view's usually good—maybe not today, though. Might be a bit drafty, but it's yours if you want it."

Whitey let out a quiet grunt of approval and took the seat by the window.

With the last of the passengers settling in, the conductor made another call of "All aboard!" before the ushers shut the doors. To Eli's relief, a crewman began stoking the cast-iron stove with coal, sending a plume of soot into the air. A few well-dressed passengers scowled at the disturbance, brushing at their coats in irritation.

Eli could tell Whitey was uneasy—his first train ride, no doubt. When the whistle blew, Whitey tensed, but as the train lurched forward, its steady chugging seemed to soothe him. He watched with quiet interest as vendors moved through the aisles, offering coffee, sandwiches, and baskets of fruit. Every so often, a man would disappear into the next car, only to return a short while later.

Noticing Whitey's curiosity, Eli explained, "That's the smoking car. It's where men go to enjoy cigars and pipes."

Whitey nodded but kept his gaze out the window, watching snow-covered pines blur past.

The usher returned, hauling another bucket of coal for the stove. Several passengers shifted away, dreading the inevitable burst of soot.

"I was about to ask if the fire needed more fuel," Eli joked. "Aren't you feeling the chill?"

Whitey didn't respond to the question. Instead, he turned from the window and asked, "How do you know this Dr. M?"

Eli noted the shift in conversation but answered anyway. "I first met Dr. McGillycuddy on the Newton Jenney Expedition back in '75. We were both surveyors, but he knew far more than I did. Taught me a lot. Afterward, he was appointed surgeon at Fort Robinson—he was the one who treated Crazy Horse after the guards fatally stabbed him."

Whitey studied Eli for a moment before saying, "I've heard of him. The Lakota call him *Putin hi chikala*—'Little Whiskers.' He was a friend of Crazy Horse."

Eli's eyebrows lifted. "That's right! Where did you hear about him?"

"There was talk of him helping to bring peace between the tribes and the army," Whitey replied.

"I wouldn't doubt that," Eli said. "You'll meet him soon enough. I think I see Rapid City in the distance."

Through the frosted glass, the growing town came into view—a bustling settlement with wooden storefronts, hotels, and saloons lining the streets. Even in the cold, the Rapid City Depot was alive with activity, wagons waiting to transport passengers and goods.

Among them was a familiar carriage.

Eli grinned as he spotted Dr. M before they even stepped off the train.

Dr. McGillycuddy greeted them quickly, his coat pulled tight against the wind. "No time for pleasantries out here—neither man nor beast should be in this weather. Let's get inside where we can speak properly."

Without argument, Eli and Whitey followed him toward the waiting carriage, bracing against the stinging cold as they prepared for the next leg of their journey.

Chapter 25 - Delayed Journey

D r. M was quick to explain that the train would not be departing any further today due to the bitter cold.

Dr. M

"I believe that," Eli said. "It was cold enough in the coach, I can't imagine how hard it would be to keep the water towers from freezing. I assume they'd add salt to the water this time of year?"

"Actually, the Chicago, Burlington & Quincy installed heaters in the tanks this year," Dr. M replied. "But they'll have to keep the engine running, or it'll freeze solid." He glanced at Eli and Whitey. "I hope you gentlemen don't mind spending the night at our home. We'll try for Buffalo Gap tomorrow—if the train is running."

"I'm actually looking forward to catching up," Eli said. "And I haven't had the pleasure of seeing your home since you finished it."

"Then it's been a long time," Dr. M said with a chuckle. "I completed the main house over a year ago."

The carriage pulled up to an impressive two-story Victorian home, its steep gabled roofs and decorative trim peeking through the snow. Constructed of wood and stone, the house had large windows and a wraparound porch that offered a grand, welcoming presence.

The McGillycuddy House

Dr. M swung the carriage door open. "Let's get inside where it's warm."

Eli and Whitey stepped down, pausing to take in the sight. A figure appeared in the large front window. Dr. M noticed and smiled. "Fanny is excited to see you, Eli."

Whitey hesitated a moment, taking in the grandeur of the house, before following Dr. M and Eli up the steps. The front door opened before they reached it.

Inside, the warmth of the house wrapped around them. Dr. M introduced Whitey to his wife. "Whitey, this is my wife, Fanny."

Fanny stepped forward and shook Whitey's hand, her eyes full of kindness. "Any friend of Eli's is a pleasure to have in our home. And they say cold hands, warm heart."

Whitey nodded awkwardly. "It's nice to meet you, ma'am. Sorry about the cold hands."

Fanny turned to Eli and gave him a warm hug. "It's been too long. How is Christina? And I bet Daniel is all grown up by now."

Eli grinned. "Christina is as fine as ever, and Daniel thinks he's grown up."

Fanny laughed.

"I promised to let Christina know we arrived safely," Eli said. "May I use your telephone?"

"Of course," Dr. M said. "Fanny, why don't you take Whitey to the parlor while Eli makes his call?"

After checking in with Christina, Eli joined the others in the parlor, where Fanny had set out coffee and cookies.

Dr. M welcomed them again and assured them he would learn more about the situation at the agency once he spoke with General Miles. Then he turned to Whitey.

"What do you think of the Spearfish area so far?"

Whitey glanced at Eli before answering. "The weather hasn't exactly been welcoming, so I haven't seen much. But I do enjoy the kindness of the Kinds."

Everyone chuckled, even Whitey.

"And I really enjoyed seeing the Anderson dairy ranch," he added.

"Oh yes," Dr. M said, smirking. "The place where Eli met his bride!"

"Technically, I met her in the smallpox tent," Eli said. "But that doesn't sound as romantic."

Dr. M laughed but quickly turned serious. "Eli, you mentioned Whitey has a personal reason for being here?"

Eli nodded. "Yes. As you can tell, he's a man of few words, so we agreed I'd explain. Before Whitey was found—by Teddy and his cowboys, no less—he spent a lot of time with the tribes. Mainly Lakota and Arikara. He believes he may have connections with the Lakota involved in the conflict."

Dr. M turned to Whitey and asked, **"Tókheča he čháŋ he?"**

Whitey gave his usual short nod. **"Hau."**

Dr. M looked back at Eli. "I asked if you were speaking the truth. He says yes."

Then he turned to Whitey again. **"IyótakA wačhíŋ kiŋ, niyákhiyA waštéwalake."**

Whitey responded, **"Na míš niyákhiyA waštéwalake."**

Dr. M nodded. "It seems we'll work well together."

The conversation shifted to the weather. "I checked with the telegraph station at the depot," Dr. M said. "The Weather Bureau says we may not get much more snow, but the wind and cold are here to stay. They're usually only right half the time, but my barometer tells me otherwise." He pointed to the gauge on the wall, its needle hovering near 'Stormy.' "I'll check with the depot in the morning."

Eli asked, "What's the plan once we leave Rapid City?"

"We'll take the Fremont, Elkhorn & Missouri Valley Railroad to Buffalo Gap," Dr. M explained. "That's about a two-hour ride. A stagecoach will take us to Rockyford, a Lakota community near the agency. From there, the army will have a military wagon to get us the rest of the way. I expect it'll take a full day's travel after we leave the train."

Later, Fanny gave Eli and Whitey a tour of the house, showing them their rooms. On their way back, they met Dr. M near the back door, bundling up.

"I need to check on my buffalo in the barn," he said. "They're used to this weather, but they're more like pets to me."

"More than pets," Fanny chimed in.

Eli offered to help. "I wouldn't mind. I've never seen a buffalo up close."

Whitey nodded. "I've been on many buffalo hunts. They are animals to be wary of."

"Not mine," Dr. M grinned. "They'll eat out of your hand."

"I'd like to see that," Whitey said, pulling on his coat.

The three men made their way to the barn, where four bison stood facing the wind. As soon as **Dr. M** entered, they turned toward him, expecting a treat.

Both Eli and Whitey soon had them eating hay straight from their hands, their warm breath clouding in the freezing air.

"Told you they were tame," Dr. M said. "They're easy to deal with—until they get an itch and lean on something."

"Planning to turn them into steaks?" Eli asked.

"No," Dr. M said. "I'm donating two live bison to the Smithsonian Institution and another to Scotty Phillips' ranch near Fort Pierre. They're working to restore the herds."

"Scotty" Phillip

Whitey nudged Eli. "I'm starting to like this guy."

Eli smiled, tossing another forkful of hay into the manger.

"That should do it," Dr. M said. "Now let's get inside before we freeze solid."

As they stripped off their heavy coats, Eli took a deep breath. "Something sure smells good."

Dr. M grinned. "I said I wouldn't turn my buffalo into dinner—but that doesn't mean I don't enjoy their cousins."

After a hearty supper fit for a king, the group retired to the parlor for more discussion.

"Did you get any more news?" Eli asked.

"No," Dr. M admitted. "This storm has everyone holed up. I'll try again in the morning."

Conversation turned to Dr. M's political ambitions, including his election to the South Dakota State Constitutional Convention and rumors of him running for mayor of Rapid City.

"I aspire to have even a fraction of your influence on this land," Eli said. "Those are big shoes to fill."

Dr. M smiled. "That means a lot, Eli."

Fanny closed the evening with a performance on the piano, filling the house with music. For a moment, the cold and the uncertainty of the coming days faded away.

Chapter 26 – Progress

The early morning silence of the McGillycuddy house was shattered by the sharp ringing of the telephone, followed by the heavy thud of Dr. M's footsteps stomping down the stairs in his nightwear. Eli and Whitey, still pulling on their clothes, were close behind.

They huddled near the phone just as the booming voice of General Nelson Miles crackled through the receiver. Though Eli and Whitey had missed the first part of the conversation, they couldn't ignore the commanding tone that even caused Dr. M to hold the receiver away from his ear.

"I don't think I can get there for a couple of days with this storm settling in," General Miles stated. "What do you think your ETA will be?"

Dr. M glanced out the window, taking in the frigid landscape. "The snow has stopped, and the wind has died down, but it's still bitterly cold. I'll check with the depot to see if the train is running today and report back."

"I'd appreciate that. And thank you for stepping up. I know things have been tense up there, and this only adds to it." There was a pause before the General continued, his voice lowering slightly. "I have a bad feeling about this one—not just because of the casualties from the fighting but also the weather. It's going to claim its own victims."

Dr. M exhaled sharply. "I agree, General. I'll be in touch shortly."

With that, the conversation ended, and Dr. M hung up the receiver. Turning to Eli and Whitey, he said, "I suppose my next call is to the depot. Let's hope someone's there."

Eli and Whitey exchanged a glance before following the scent of fresh coffee into the kitchen, where Fanny McGillycuddy greeted them with a warm smile, already holding up the pot.

"Good morning, gentlemen!" she said cheerfully, motioning to the cups hanging on the wall. "Did you sleep well—at least until that wretched ringing woke you?"

Whitey extended his cup with a mumble. "Yes, ma'am."

Eli took his own cup and grinned. "I slept great, Fanny. You have a wonderful home."

Fanny beamed. "Thank you, Eli. I've heard plenty about yours as well, and I still need to see it someday."

"You most certainly do!" Eli replied.

Just then, Dr. M entered the kitchen. "The train is scheduled to leave for Buffalo Gap at nine. We'd best start gathering our things."

The trio set off from the McGillycuddy house in a carriage, bundled against the bitter morning cold. As they rolled through Rapid City, Eli took note of something peculiar about the house's positioning.

"Dr. M, why did you build your house at an angle to the streets behind it?" he asked, pointing out the window.

Dr. M chuckled. "I was wondering when your surveying instincts would kick in." He shook his head. "It's actually a bit embarrassing. When I started building, I assumed the city planners had everything lined up properly. Turns out, they laid out the streets according to magnetic north instead of true north."

Eli questioned. "So Rapid City's original layout was off by about… ten degrees?"

Dr. M grinned. "Close—eleven degrees, to be exact. But I'll give it to you."

Whitey, listening intently, furrowed his brow. "Are we taking a different route to the depot?"

Dr. M nodded. "Yes. This time, we're heading to the Fremont, Elkhorn & Missouri Valley Depot. I picked you up at the Chicago, Burlington & Quincy Depot."

Eli raised an eyebrow. "I didn't realize Rapid City had two train depots. This place is really growing."

Dr. M smiled. "That it is. And here we are."

The three men stepped down from the carriage, the bitter wind biting through their coats, and grabbed their weapons before heading toward the Fremont, Elkhorn & Missouri Valley Passenger Station.

"We need to check our weapons with the conductor on this railroad," Dr. M informed them.

Eli hesitated, glancing at Dr. M with concern.

"It's just a formality," Dr. M assured him. "You'll see."

There was a short line at the ticket counter, and once their tickets were secured, they approached the conductor, who simply waved them through without issue.

"Told you," Dr. M murmured as they boarded the train.

The usual "All aboard!" rang out, and with a jolt, the train lurched forward, heading down the track.

Inside, the first-class coach was noticeably warmer than their previous journey.

"I feel spoiled," Eli admitted, stretching out on the padded bench seat. "Though I think our last coach was a bit fancier, this one is certainly warmer."

Dr. M grinned. "Only the best for you, Eli."

"So, with any luck, we should make it to Buffalo Gap by 11 today, correct?" Eli asked Dr. M.

"That's the plan," Dr. M confirmed. "Lieutenant Dunbar will meet us at the depot in Buffalo Gap and brief us on what he knows from the battlefield. I hope to reach Rockyford before dark, where we'll stay the night, then press on to the battlefield the following day."

Eli leaned forward. "Do you have any thoughts on what actually happened?"

Dr. M sighed, rubbing his chin. "I do. I've felt the tension growing ever since Crazy Horse was killed at Fort Robinson. He could have helped guide his people toward a better path than war. He didn't want life on a reservation, but he understood that the alternative was worse."

Eli met his gaze. "You were there, weren't you?"

Dr. M nodded solemnly. "Yes. At first, I didn't think the stab wound would kill him. But it was worse than I realized."

Whitey remained silent, staring out at the passing Black Hills, but Eli could tell he was listening intently.

Dr. M continued. "The tension only grew worse when the Lakota began practicing the Ghost Dance."

Eli frowned. "I've heard of it, but I don't know much about it."

Dr. M nodded. "It was introduced by a Paiute spiritual leader named Wovoka—also known as Jack Wilson—after he claimed to have a vision during a solar eclipse in '89. He believed it was a message from God. The dance was meant to be a peaceful spiritual movement, a way for the spirits of their ancestors to reunite with the living, restoring the old way of life."

Dr. M paused, his expression darkening. "But to many, it became something else—a rallying cry. Tribes gathered in greater numbers. Warriors began to believe the dance would make them invulnerable to bullets. The army took that as a direct threat. Orders came down to put a stop to it."

Eli listened carefully as Dr. M continued. "About a month ago, General Miles shared a telegram with me from Governor Millette of South Dakota. It was about Scotty Phillips, the rancher I told you about. He and others reported that hundreds of cattle were being stolen or killed by warriors gathering in the Badlands. Soldiers were afraid to enter, fearing ambush. Millette wanted to muster a company of cowboys to recover the stolen cattle and push back the warriors. He also warned that a growing number of men were performing the Ghost Dance, believing in its supposed powers."

Eli nodded as Dr. M continued. "One of Wovoka's followers, a man named Short Bull, convinced the Lakota that the dance would make them immune to bullets. White settlers feared it would lead to an uprising. The authorities believed Sitting Bull was the movement's leader, so they sent Indian police to arrest him, thinking it would put an end to it."

Dr. M sighed. "They arrived before dawn at his cabin. A struggle broke out between his followers and the police. Lieutenant Bull Head and Sergeant Red Tomahawk shot him in the head and chest, killing him instantly. Several others were killed in the chaos."

Suddenly, Whitey shot up in his seat, his eyes wide. "Sitting Bull is dead?"

Both Eli and Dr. M turned, startled by his outburst.

"Did you know him?" Eli asked cautiously.

Whitey swayed slightly as the train rocked along the tracks, his voice tight with emotion. "First Crazy Horse... now Sitting Bull. Who is left?" He clenched his fists. "They were great leaders... great warriors."

Dr. M placed a steady hand on Whitey's shoulder. "Yes, they were. And now, I fear this will only get worse."

Eli straightened. "What do you mean?"

Dr. M exhaled. "After Sitting Bull was killed, Chief Big Foot took about 350 Lakota and fled south toward Pine Ridge, most likely seeking protection under Red Cloud. The U.S. Army pursued them. That's where we are now."

Eli's expression hardened. "So the battle we're going to… it's likely what happened when the army caught up with Big Foot and his people?"

Dr. M nodded grimly. "I'm afraid so."

Whitey slowly sank back into his seat. His eyes swept the train car before returning to the window, his expression unreadable.

Eli wanted to say something—offer some kind of comfort—but he knew Whitey well enough now to give him space.

The three men sat in silence as the train rumbled along.

Not long after, the usher came through, tossing coal into the stove to warm the car. "Buffalo Gap coming up!" he announced.

At the Buffalo Gap depot, the bitter cold bit at their faces as they stepped onto the platform. Lieutenant Dunbar was waiting for them. After a brief greeting, he led them inside a small office.

"I assume General Miles has already brought you up to speed?" Dunbar asked, his expression grim.

Dr. M nodded. "I know the basics. What can you add?"

Dunbar exhaled. "The situation is worse than we feared. We estimate over 300 casualties—most of them Lakota."

Dr. M's jaw tightened. "Were you there?"

"No, sir," Dunbar admitted. "I was stationed at Rockyford. We thought another uprising would happen there, but it didn't. The battle took place about 30 miles south. Some of the wounded soldiers made it to Rockyford before the blizzard hit. We treated them as best we could before bringing them here once the weather cleared."

He gestured out the window. They could see wounded soldiers being loaded onto the train.

Dr. M asked, "Can I speak with any of them?"

Dunbar shook his head. "I'm sorry, sir. My orders are to take you to the battlefield immediately. There are still people there who need help."

Dr. M set his jaw and nodded. "Then let's not waste any time."

The men bundled up under heavy blankets as they climbed into the stagecoach. The wind had eased, but the frigid air still gnawed at them as the stage rumbled eastward, away from the shadow of the Black Hills.

The road was rough, the ride jarring. Lieutenant Dunbar advised them, "It'll be difficult, but try to rest while you can. The next stop won't be a peaceful one."

By the time they reached Rockyford, darkness had already fallen. Dunbar led them to a small shack, once a granary, now converted into a bunkhouse.

Dinner consisted of army rations—salted beef, beans, and coffee. It was far from a feast, but no one was in the mood to complain.

Before turning in for the night, Dr. M looked at Eli and Whitey, his face etched with concern.

179

"Tomorrow, we'll see firsthand what happened."

Eli exchanged a glance with Whitey, whose face remained shadowed by the dim lantern light.

No one said another word.

Sleep did not come easily.

Chapter 27 - On to the Battlefield

As predicted by Dunbar, sleep was hard to come by in the converted bunkhouse. The only positive was that since no one could sleep well, there was always someone awake to feed the little pot-bellied stove, keeping it from going out completely. By the time Eli and Whitey made their way outside, Dr. M had already been up for hours, gathering provisions and convincing the stagecoach driver to take them the rest of the way. This way, they would not have to endure the rough ride in the army wagon. When they climbed aboard, Dr. M handed them cornbread and more salted beef for the journey.

Eli thanked Dr. M for the breakfast and asked, "I overheard someone refer to the battlefield as Wounded Knee. Do you know anything about that name?"

Dr. M, caught mid-bite of cornbread, raised a finger while he chewed and swallowed. "Yes," he finally answered. "The battle took place near a creek called Wounded Knee."

"Seems like an odd name for a creek," Eli remarked.

"I thought the same," Dr. M agreed. "One of the Lakota scouts in the wagon behind us said it was named after an injury suffered near the creek. Over time, the name stuck and became official."

"So we're heading to the Wounded Knee Battlefield then?" Eli questioned.

"It would seem that is now the accepted designation," Dr. M confirmed.

As the sun rose, its warmth penetrated the frosted windows of the stagecoach. A light dusting of morning snow was swept off the grass as the coach pressed on, with Lieutenant Dunbar leading ten army wagons behind them. They were only a few miles from Wounded Knee when they encountered an army patrol. Dunbar stopped to exchange words with them before signaling for the convoy to continue.

Dr. M called out to the stagecoach driver. "Pull up alongside Dunbar."

When the coach reached him, Dr. M leaned out the door. "Are they part of the Seventh?" he asked.

"Yes," Dunbar replied. "They're patrolling the area, gathering the dead and looking for survivors. We're close now—you'll be seeing more patrols."

Dr. M sat back inside, his expression darkening. Eli, sensing the shift, asked cautiously, "Did you say the Seventh?"

"Yes they came from Fort Meade, why?" Dr. M started to ask, then realization dawned. "That was your cavalry under Custer, wasn't it?"

Eli nodded grimly. "This doesn't feel right at all."

He looked down at the floor of the stage, shaking his head in unease. Just then, the coach came to an abrupt halt.

Through the window, Eli saw why—a wagon, piled with frozen bodies, was passing by. The corpses, twisted and contorted in the positions they had fallen, were covered in bloodstained clothing, stiff from the bitter cold. The sight was gruesome.

Dr. M, Eli, and Whitey sat in stunned silence, their eyes fixed on the horrific display. Dr. M was the first to break the silence. He leaned out of the stage and asked the driver, "How much farther?"

"Just over the next hill, where the fires are burning," the driver responded.

Eli leaned out the opposite door, watching the smoke rise in the distance. "That can't be from the battle. The village wouldn't still be burning."

As they crested the hill, the source of the smoke became clear. Fires had been built in one area, with soldiers adding more wood to the flames. They were close enough now to see what remained of the village.

What lay before them was a sight none of them would ever forget.

The snow-covered prairie was stained with blood. Bodies of Lakota men, women, and children were frozen where they had fallen, their faces twisted in agony. Scattered across the battlefield were the remnants of their lives—blankets, cooking utensils, weapons— abandoned in the chaos. Deep snowdrifts partially covered the dead, but the horror was still visible.

The stagecoach stopped in front of an army tent, smoke curling from its stovepipe. Dr. M, Eli, and Whitey climbed down and were met by Colonel James W. Forsyth, the commander of the Seventh Cavalry.

"Dr. McGillycuddy," Forsyth greeted him. "A pleasure to meet you, though I wish it were under different circumstances."

Dr. M nodded solemnly as Forsyth turned to Eli. "Eli Kind, I heard you might be coming. I've heard good things about you."

Eli acknowledged him with a nod. Forsyth then extended his hand to Whitey, who hesitated before reluctantly shaking it.

"I don't believe we've met," Forsyth said.

Dr. M interjected, "This is my guest, Whitey. He has extensive experience with the Lakota and other tribes. I believe he'll be a valuable asset in understanding what truly happened here."

Forsyth motioned them toward a wooden table with several chairs. "Please, sit. I'll explain the situation."

They settled in, and Forsyth took a deep breath before beginning. "After the death of Sitting Bull, we were ordered to track the group that left the Standing Rock Reservation, led by Big Foot. We intercepted them here at Wounded Knee to prevent them from joining Red Cloud's people at Pine Ridge. The following morning, I ordered the disarmament of the tribe, as we had intelligence that an uprising was imminent. During the initial search, it became evident they were hiding weapons."

Forsyth's jaw tightened. "A second search was ordered, which angered the tribe. A man by the name of Sits Straight began performing the Ghost Dance, attempting to rally the others, claiming their sacred ghost shirts would protect them from bullets. As his dance grew frenzied, tensions rose. I ordered my men to stand down, but then— shots rang out. Within minutes, it turned into a full-scale battle. The smoke, the chaos… it was impossible to tell who was who. And you've seen the result."

Just then, a thunderous explosion shook the ground.

Eli instinctively reached for his sidearm. Dr. M and Whitey threw themselves to the ground.

"Stand down!" Forsyth said quickly. "That was my men. We've been using dynamite to loosen the frozen ground for graves. Fires have been burning for over a day, but it's barely making a difference. Major Miles sent reinforcements after we were ambushed in retaliation. But the area is secure now."

Dr. M dusted himself off and asked, "Are there any wounded in need of immediate attention?"

"Unclear," Forsyth admitted. "Injured soldiers were sent back to Rapid City yesterday, and the Lakota wounded were taken to Pine Ridge Agency. But in the chaos, there may still be survivors out there."

Dr. M's expression hardened. "The cold alone will have done damage. We need to get to work."

Forsyth nodded. "Then let's begin."

With that, Eli, Whitey, and Dr. M stepped back into the frozen aftermath of Wounded Knee, bracing themselves for what lay ahead.

Chapter 28 - The Aftermath

D
r. M wasted no time setting up a makeshift infirmary in an army tent, tending to the injured. Most of the wounds were frostbite-related, made worse by men who mistakenly believed that rubbing snow or ice on the affected areas would help, when in reality, it only caused further damage.

Meanwhile, Eli, Whitey, and other hired civilians assisted in the grim task of recovering bodies scattered across the remnants of the village. It was a job worse than anything they could have imagined. Many of the frozen corpses had to be pried from the hardened ground, their limbs contorted in the positions of their final moments. Loading them onto wagons in such a state was no easy task.

Despite efforts to prepare the burial site, progress was slow. The grave diggers had set fires on the ground to soften it, even resorting to dynamite, yet the trench they managed to carve out was barely three feet deep.

Whitey, brushing snow off a body, suddenly stopped and recoiled. He crouched back down, examining the face beneath the frost. His breath came in quick, visible puffs as he called out, "Eli, come here!"

Eli, who was maneuvering a wagon closer, jumped down and hurried over.

"What is it?" he asked.

Whitey looked up, his frost-covered beard barely concealing the concern in his face. "It's Chief Big Foot."

Eli frowned. "Are you sure?"

"Yes," Whitey said firmly. "I hunted buffalo with him when he was younger. I knew him as *Si Tȟaŋka*—Spotted Elk."

The chief's body lay twisted in the snow, frozen in time, as if he had been trying to rise, his fingers still pointing in a direction away from the massacre.

Whitey knelt beside him, mumbling something Eli didn't understand—perhaps a prayer. Eli gave him a moment, stepping away to scan the battlefield. Wagons continued to roll through the scene of devastation, collecting the dead.

Turning back, he saw Whitey struggling with the chief's body. Eli rushed to help, but Whitey stopped suddenly, letting go.

"I can't do this," Whitey muttered, his voice shaking. "None of them deserved this. And now, tossing them into a mass grave... I won't do it."

Eli understood. Whitey was shaken to his core, and so was he.

"I get it," Eli said, his voice low. "But I don't think the Colonel has another option right now." He glanced toward the burial site. "I can take the wagon up to Sergeant Bell and come back with another. I know that's not much of a solution, but—"

Whitey sighed, rubbing his face. "Fine. I'll keep working, but I won't be part of burying them like that."

Together, they carefully lifted Big Foot's body into the wagon. They stood there for a moment, staring at the chief's aged, weathered face before Eli climbed onto the wagon, and Whitey walked off toward the western edge of the village.

There, Whitey noticed a man setting up a tripod with a wooden box mounted on top. He kept his distance, not wanting to engage. When Eli returned with an empty wagon, a voice called out to them.

"Would you be willing to be in a photograph?"

Eli turned to see the man with the tripod, his hand extended.

"Name's George Trager. I'm a photographer."

Eli shook his hand but quickly shook his head. "No disrespect, but I don't want to be in any pictures here."

Trager nodded. "What about your friend?"

Eli glanced at Whitey, who was watching from a short distance. "No. I'm sure he'd object even more than I would."

"I understand," Trager said. "This is a tragedy, but if we don't document it, people will forget."

Eli sighed. "You're right. What happened here *shouldn't* be forgotten. But I still don't want my picture taken."

Trager didn't argue. "I already have most of what I need," he said, adjusting the glass plate on his camera. "I just want one more shot of the guns on the hill."

Eli and Whitey watched as he finished his preparations, adjusting the tripod's legs and removing the lens cap. After a few seconds, he capped the lens again and packed up his gear.

"It was nice meeting you, Eli," Trager said as he gathered his equipment.

"You too," Eli replied, watching him trudge up the snow-covered hill.

Whitey, still staring at the hilltop, suddenly asked, "What are those up there?"

Eli followed his gaze. The long black barrels of the weapons gleamed in the sunlight, their wooden wheels partially blocking the full view.

"Hotchkiss machine guns," Eli said grimly. "Probably the most powerful weapons in the army's arsenal. And, I'd guess, the main reason for all of this." He gestured toward the field of bodies.

Whitey muttered something under his breath, his expression dark, before walking off to continue the gruesome work.

By sundown, Eli and Whitey were relieved to see Dr. M approaching.

"I need your help setting up tents," Dr. M said. "We'll be staying the night. The Colonel wants a morning briefing before we leave."

Eli exhaled heavily. He wanted to be far away from this place, but at least the work was nearly done.

As they walked back toward the army camp, they passed a group of soldiers huddled around a fire, warming themselves. The men looked up and fell silent as Eli, Whitey, and Dr M walked by, but once they realized they were just civilians, their conversation resumed.

Once at camp, they got to work setting up their tents and stoking fires in the iron stoves. The temperature was dropping fast.

As the flames flickered, casting shadows against the canvas walls, Eli sat in silence, staring into the fire. The day's horrors weighed on him, and the thought of what they had witnessed—and what it meant—settled deep in his chest.

Tomorrow, they would leave this place. But the memory of Wounded Knee would never leave them.

Chapter 29 – Concerns

D r M joined Eli and Whitey in their tent after speaking with Colonel Forsyth and Major Whitside. Eli and Whitey had both pushed their cots closer to the stove for warmth, and Dr. M followed suit, moving his in closer.

Breaking the silence, Dr. M sighed, "Quite the day, gentlemen. One we may want to forget, but one we should never allow to happen again."

Eli nodded while Whitey remained quiet, staring into the crackling fire.

"I truly want to thank you both for coming here to help," Dr. M continued. "I'll make sure you're fully compensated for your time."

Eli looked up, about to speak, but Dr. M cut him off. "I know what you're going to say, Eli, but I insist. I also need your help piecing this together. I've heard the officers' version, but there are missing pieces."

Eli furrowed his brow. "What do you think is missing?"

Dr. M hesitated. "Maybe 'missing' isn't the right word. This might sound harsh, but... do you believe this was a battle or a slaughter?"

Eli looked up, meeting Dr. M's eyes. He paused before answering. "This is hard for me to admit. I served with many of the officers here. I know the deep resentment they carry from Little Bighorn—the scars are still raw. The connection between these events is deeply personal and tragic. That said, I can't condone what happened here. Yes... I believe it was a slaughter."

Dr. M let out a slow breath. "Have you heard anything about the 7th Cavalry's casualties?"

"I haven't," Eli admitted. "Have you?"

"Yes," Dr. M replied. "I was told there were around 25 dead, with several more injured."

Eli exhaled sharply. "Last I was at the gravesite, I heard the number of Lakota dead was at least 200—including Chief Big Foot."

Dr. M's eyes widened. "Chief Big Foot was among the casualties?"

"Yes," Eli confirmed. "Whitey identified him. I told Sergeant Bell to report it to the Colonel, but apparently, that didn't happen?"

Dr. M's voice grew tight with frustration. "Not that I've heard. That will be my first question at the briefing tomorrow."

Whitey, who had been sitting silently, suddenly stood up, his face tense with anger. "I knew they were just going to throw him in a hole and forget about him!" His voice trembled with rage. "And yes, it was a slaughter! Did you not hear the soldiers bragging about how the Indians exploded when they fired down on them from the ridge?"

Dr. M's expression turned grim. "You mean the German soldiers who stopped talking when we passed?"

"Yes," Whitey said bitterly. "They only stopped because they thought we were officers. Once they realized we weren't, they started telling their gruesome stories about firing down on the Indians."

Eli's jaw tightened. "So, the Hotchkiss artillery rounds were explosive?"

Dr. M nodded. "Yes. Using all four of them at once… it would have been hell on the other end."

"It sure was," Eli said through clenched teeth. "What can we do?"

Dr. M looked at Whitey, who had sunk back into his seat in silent fury, then turned back to Eli. "We need to get the truth out about what happened here. Do you two have any more information I should relay to the Colonel tomorrow?"

Eli hesitated, then lowered his head. "There is something else," he said, glancing up. "Why were some of the warriors stripped of their clothing?"

Dr. M, who had started adjusting his cot in preparation for sleep, stopped and turned back to Eli. "I was told soldiers were taking their Ghost Dance shirts. They believed the shirts had mystical powers— supposedly, they could stop bullets." He shook his head. "The Colonel assured me he put a stop to it and that anyone found with one would be punished."

Eli exhaled. "So, the Ghost Dance really had the soldiers spooked?"

Dr. M nodded solemnly. "It seems the Ghost Dance had a lot to do with this massacre."

Eli and Dr. M settled into their cots, but Whitey remained seated, still staring into the fire, long after the lamps had been extinguished.

Chapter 30 - Leaving Wounded Knee

The next morning, all three men were up early. Dr. M prepared his notes while Eli and Whitey found breakfast at the makeshift army mess hall. Whitey remained silent, and Eli was beginning to worry about him.

The camp was bustling as soldiers tore down tents and loaded supplies onto wagons. What had once been used to haul bodies was now being repurposed to carry the remaining provisions. Dr. M assured Eli and Whitey that they would be heading out within the hour. They wouldn't be taking the stagecoach this time, as it was scheduled to meet them at Rockyford. Instead, they would endure the rough ride in one of the wagons. Eli cringed at the thought but quickly reminded himself that he was far better off than the poor souls he had witnessed at Wounded Knee.

The wagon trail back to Rockyford was just as rough as Eli had imagined, but at least the weather had warmed up, making the journey more bearable. As promised, the stage was waiting for them at Rockyford, and they were quick to board, heading west toward the train station in Buffalo Gap. Dr. M pushed the driver to make good time, ensuring they would meet the 8 PM departure. They reached the platform just as the conductor called out the familiar, "All aboard!"

The comfort of the padded train seats was a welcome relief after such a long and grueling journey. Whitey, still silent except for the occasional grunt, took a seat at the back of the coach, pressing himself against the window.

Eli, seated across from Dr. M, leaned in and spoke in a low voice. "I'm really worried about Whitey. I think Wounded Knee was too much for him."

Dr. M nodded. "I've been concerned too. I want to help him, but I don't know much about his past."

Eli glanced toward Whitey, then got up to sit closer to Dr. M. Keeping his voice low, he said, "Whitey's a bit of a mystery to me as well, but I feel I owe you an explanation—and honestly, I may need your help."

Eli recounted everything he knew about Whitey: his time with the tribes, his work with Teddy Roosevelt, and his connection to the Thoen Stone. When he mentioned the caves and their possible link to Whitey's past, Dr. M suddenly interrupted.

"Wait a minute," Dr. M said, eyes narrowing. "I have to admit, when I first met Whitey, I was convinced he was related to you. His eyes, his build—it's uncanny. And those writings you mentioned? I want to see them."

"You're not the first to notice the resemblance," Eli admitted. "Christina was the first to point it out, and she still believes it. I do too, but Whitey just doesn't remember. I'd take him to the spot where the Thoen Stone was found, but the snow is too deep right now."

Dr. M rubbed his chin thoughtfully. "The mind is a complex tapestry of thoughts, emotions, and memories—constantly weaving together perception and reality. Whitey's memory issues are a puzzle, but I think I might have found another piece."

Eli frowned. "What do you mean?"

Dr. M lowered his voice even more. "Remember last night when Whitey told us about the soldiers talking about the Hotchkiss guns?"

"Yeah, why?" Eli asked.

Dr. M hesitated before saying, "At first, I didn't understand why I hadn't picked up on what they were saying... then I realized—it's because they were speaking German."

Eli's eyes widened. He glanced at Whitey, then turned back to Dr. M. "Do you think Whitey understands German?"

"He has to," Dr. M said. "That's the only way he would have understood their conversation."

Eli thought back to his own childhood. "My father was from Germany, but my mother wasn't. She never spoke the language, but I remember calling my sister 'Arschloch' when I was little, and I got in a lot of trouble for it. I'd heard my dad say it when he was angry, so I thought I could use it too. My uncle Richard, who came to live with us later, spoke German with my father a lot, but I never picked up much. They did let us get away with calling each other 'Dummkopf,' though."

Dr. M chuckled. "I'm not trying to get your hopes up, but Whitey learning German while living with the tribes seems... unlikely."

Before they could discuss further, the train usher entered the coach, announcing their arrival in Rapid City. At the sound of the station name, Whitey straightened up and started looking around.

Dr. M turned to Eli. "I made arrangements for a ride to the CB&Q station. They are still trying to catch up from the weather cancelations so they will be running late tonight. You're welcome to stay the night, but I assume you'd rather get home?"

"Yeah, I'd like to get back," Eli confirmed.

Dr. M nodded, then looked toward Whitey. "And I assume the same from him, but I'll ask."

The train came to a jerking stop, nearly knocking Dr. M off balance. Regaining his footing, he approached Whitey. "You're welcome to stay at my home again, or I can take you to the station for the next train to Whitewood."

Whitey let out a short grunt that sounded like a yes to leaving on the next train.

"Alright then," Dr. M said. "We'll get you there."

Outside the station, Dr. M's buggy was waiting at the end of the platform. They climbed in for the short ride to the Chicago, Burlington & Quincy station. After securing their tickets, Dr. M turned to Eli.

"Eli, I can't thank you enough for your dedication during this tragedy. I'll be in touch if I need anything more from you, and I'll let you know if I learn anything new."

Eli shook his hand firmly. "Thank you, Dr. M. You have a lot on your shoulders—don't hesitate to reach out."

Dr. M pulled Eli into a brief but heartfelt hug. "I won't, my friend."

He then turned to Whitey, extending his hand. Whitey shook it without a word.

"It's been a pleasure working with you, Whitey," Dr. M said sincerely. "I hope our paths cross again."

Whitey nodded but remained silent.

Dr. M took a step back. "I realize nothing about this trip was enjoyable, but it was important. As terrible as it was, I do believe this marks the end of the Indian Wars. Hopefully, it will be a time for reflection and reconciliation." He gave a final nod. "Safe travels to you both—I hope to see you again soon."

"You will," Eli assured him.

Whitey simply turned toward the platform, watching as passengers boarded the train.

Eli made his way to the station telephone, calling Christina to let her know that he and Whitey would be arriving in Whitewood. As he hung up, the familiar call rang through the station—"All aboard!"

Eli and Whitey boarded their coach and settled into their seats across from each other. After a long silence, Eli finally spoke.

"Whitey… is there something wrong? Something I can help with?"

Whitey stared out the window for a moment, then met Eli's gaze. "There's a lot wrong… and I'm not sure if there's a way to help. I just need time."

Eli hesitated, unsure how to respond. Finally, he stammered, "I understand."

Nothing more was said. The only sound was the rhythmic clatter of the train wheels as they carried them home.

Chapter 31 - Back Home

As the train neared the Whitewood station, Eli spotted Christina and Daniel standing on the dimly lit platform. Though exhausted from the long day of travel, the sight of his family gave him a sudden burst of energy.

With few passengers on the late train, it didn't take long for Eli and Whitey to step onto the platform and into the welcoming arms of Christina and Daniel. It was nearly midnight, and after hugs and warm greetings, Eli turned to his son.

"Thank you for coming with your mother to get us, but we'd better get home soon—it's a school night."

Daniel smiled. "I know, Dad, but I'll be fine. We're only learning about fractions, and who needs to be awake for that?"

The night was mild for January, but the extra blankets in the buggy were welcome. The ride home was filled with Daniel's chatter about how he kept up with the chores and took care of the livestock in the bitter cold. He described how one day, he built a fire on top of the water tank just to melt the ice enough to chip through it.

"I didn't get too many black coals in the water, and the cows didn't mind anyway," he said proudly.

Eli chuckled. "That was pretty smart, Daniel. How'd you come up with that?"

Daniel hesitated before confessing, "I saw Grandpa James do it once on the creek in the pasture."

Eli and Christina laughed, giving Daniel credit for his resourcefulness. Daniel glanced at Whitey, hoping for a reaction, but Whitey remained silent the entire ride home.

When they reached the barn, Eli instructed everyone to head inside and get some rest—he would take care of the horse and buggy. Christina and Daniel took him up on the offer, but Whitey stayed behind, still saying nothing. Eli considered pressing him for conversation but decided against it. If Whitey wanted silence, Eli would give it to him. Maybe by morning, he'd be ready to talk.

After putting the tack away, Eli wished Whitey goodnight as he headed inside. He got the usual grunt in response, which, to Eli, was at least something.

Before he could climb into bed, Christina asked, "What's wrong with Whitey? He barely said two words the whole way home, and he didn't even react to Daniel's story."

Eli sighed. "I know. He's been like that for days. The things we saw out there… they're hard to explain, even harder to justify. I think it's taken a toll on him—on both of us. But he's holding it all in."

Christina reached for his hand. "I know it's late, and you've had some long days, but come join me. I've missed you."

Eli settled into bed beside her, but their rest was soon disturbed by the sound of shuffling feet and the creak of a door closing.

"Is that Whitey? What time is it?" Christina murmured.

Eli glanced at the clock. "Yeah, I think so. It's four in the morning. I'll go check."

Throwing on a coat, Eli stepped outside and spotted a light on in the barn. Through the window, he could see Whitey saddling his horse and securing his saddlebags.

Eli pushed open the barn door. "What's going on, Whitey?"

Without turning, Whitey replied, "It's time I go back where I belong."

"You mean back to Elkhorn?"

"Yes."

Eli hesitated. "Did I do something to upset you?"

Whitey tightened his saddle straps. "No, not at all. You and your family have been the kindest people I've ever met. I just need to go back."

"Can't you stay a few more days? Dr. M is sending some money to you through Western Union—it should be here today or tomorrow."

"No. You keep it. I don't want his money."

Eli started to protest but stopped himself, realizing there was no changing Whitey's mind.

"At least stay for breakfast," he tried. "Christina and Daniel will want to say goodbye."

Whitey finally turned to face Eli. His expression was tight, his eyes glassy. "It would be too hard. I didn't want to wake anyone."

Eli felt a deep sadness settle in. Too much had been left unsaid—some of it his fault for never asking. Now, the only tie he had left to his family's mystery was slipping away.

"Will you come back? Maybe after calving season, when the weather is nicer?"

Whitey led his horse outside and swung into the saddle. Looking down at Eli, he hesitated before answering. "Yeah. I feel like there's something here... but I need time."

"I understand."

A memory surfaced in Eli's mind—his father and Uncle Richard, speaking German to one another. They had always shared a phrase, passing it between them like a game.

As Whitey nudged his horse forward, Eli called out, **"Das Leben ist kein Ponyhof."**

Without turning, Whitey lifted his arm and replied, **"You're right. Ade, Eli."**

Thank you for taking part in The Kind Legacy Series. Till next time remember, "Life is not a pony farm!"